SILENTLY

TRANSFORMATION SERIES
BOOK 1

TALYA BLAINE

Ebook ISBN-13: 978-1-959336-00-6

Paperback ISBN-13: 978-1-959336-03-7

To M.

TABLE OF CONTENTS

1

GHOST

Through the wall of bedroom windows, Quinn looked down on the polished sports cars, oversized SUVs, and black sedans that, once again, lined the circular pea stone drive. Just like after Harris's funeral thirteen months ago, wisps of cigarette smoke from the waiting chauffeurs wafted up and in through the screen. Beyond the narrow private road at the end of the drive, dunes held fast to their beach grasses, cleaved by the rickety boardwalk that led to the sea. Twilight infused the peach and lavender sky with a streak of red where it met the Atlantic.

She should join the guests downstairs, at least for a while, although all she wanted was for this evening to be over. But she had consented a few weeks ago, and she did not want to disappoint Leigh.

The disaster now occupying the main floor of her home had all been her agent's idea. Leigh, who had become a close friend in the fifteen years she represented Quinn, originally proposed some kind of "life celebration."

No way.

In a few months, or years, perhaps, but not now.

Instead, she agreed to a small, informal get-together for wine and cheese. "All you'll have to do is put on something that's not those yoga pants and come downstairs," Leigh had said.

How that translated to a catered, strolling affair for forty and a jazz ensemble, Quinn was not sure. One thing was clear: Leigh was on a mission to drag her out of the deep, tarry funk of grief that mired her and, among so many other things, kept her from finishing her next book.

She descended the back stairs to the kitchen, nodding at the caterers arranging tapas on rustic olive wood trays. If she emerged from the kitchen rather than from the direction of the winding main stairway, the guests would assume she had been among them the whole time.

Before leaving the kitchen, she took a small plate from the stack on the counter and put two crackers on it. Then she picked up a bottle of Chardonnay—better, Merlot—and poured a glass. With her hands full, with red wine no less, no one would try to hug her. She had grown weary of so many awkward attempts at comfort and affection.

As she headed from the safety of the kitchen to the living room, trying to keep her gaze downcast, a waving hand shot up from a circle of guests. There was no mistaking that wide band of bangles on the wrist. *Leigh.*

Although Quinn couldn't hear the bracelets' jangle over the Coltrane or the din of conversation, she moved toward it.

"Quinn, you remember . . ." Leigh reintroduced her to their more distant circle of acquaintances. She imagined Leigh rounding them up, calling in favors for this pointless show of support, although all she wanted was to be left alone. *Yes, yes, of course I remember.* Nods and forced smiles. *How nice of you to come.*

One by one they moved closer to embrace her—loosely; the wine glass worked like a charm—and pat-pat her back.

It had become familiar, this widow Morse code. *Poor thing. Now, time for you to move on.* Pat. *Because we don't know what to say to you and it's getting uncomfortable.* Pat.

Women always gave two pats. *There, there.* Like she was an inconsolable child. Some men would add a third—pat-pat, pat. Two shorts and a long—*if you ever get lonely*—that would linger awkwardly until she pulled away.

The last person Leigh turned to, the man who had been hanging back coolly, respectfully, Quinn already knew. Jonathan Jaines, Explore Network's *Spice of Life* foodie travel show host.

The director of the screen adaptation of Quinn's last novel had brought him in to consult when they shot the movie three years ago. Tonight, bleeding dye from the cocktail napkin around his sweating beer bottle left the swirl of his thumb blue, as if he'd been fingerprinted.

On the inside of his wrist, she spied a simple tattoo: *Dare.* Four spare characters in handwritten lettering, no decoration, like he had jotted a quick reminder: Pick up milk, eggs, bread.

He didn't have it when they worked together, she was sure. It was an intense couple of weeks; she would have noticed.

She wondered, what was it he wanted to do—the man traveled the world; he seemed to have a great life—and what was holding him back?

Without a word or a step toward her, he smiled, the skin at the corners of his warm brown eyes wrinkling—eyes that held empathy, not pity. After more than a year, she could discern the two.

His hair had grayed at the temples. His teeth were still bleached for TV and, up close, slightly, boyishly, crooked.

The others around the room noticed her, and they came toward her in the same slow-motion haze she could not shake these last months. As if her body were present but her mind observed from a distance, like she was listening to some audiobook, volume low, one earbud dangling rather than in her ear.

It wouldn't matter if an earthquake rumbled right beneath her feet—it would probably feel like it was unfolding a million miles away.

And now the guests, their voices distant, asked her questions that were impossible to answer: *How are you? What have you been up to? How's the writing?*

Writing. If one day she remembered how to laugh again, she would laugh at this. As if she had written a single sentence since that afternoon.

Already she needed to get away. "Excuse me," she said to the group but looked at him, the understanding face in the crowd, the one that didn't feel so far away.

She turned and hurried back to the kitchen, playing a proper hostess rushing to fetch something for a waiting guest. This way, no one would waylay her with more impossible questions.

The door swung closed behind her and she slowed, nodded at the catering staff again, and climbed the back stairs.

In the isolation of her study, she sat back in the armchair, put her feet on the ottoman, and drew the quiet around her like a blanket.

Soon they would all leave; the house would be empty again. In the near darkness, she traced the two hearts of the pendant at her neck with her fingertips. It would be thuddingly empty.

After a while, voices down the hall murmured. The sounds came closer, and she stood and darted into the dark alcove by the closet, just in case. The hum of the voices separated into words, then sentences.

"And this is her office."

Are you kidding? Leigh was giving a tour? She tried to quiet her breathing. Why hadn't she closed the door behind her? She could edge her way into the closet, but they would hear the door slide. It had been binding forever—how many times had she meant to ask Harris to oil the rails?

"How can she stand staying here?" a woman's voice she didn't recognize asked.

"Just tragic," echoed another, familiar but unrecognizable.

Mm. Tsk. Cluck. Utterances of sympathy and fear. But mostly, of relief at their own good fortune—it had been someone else's husband, not theirs.

The sounds stopped mid-conversation. "Quinn?" Leigh's surprised voice asked.

Quinn sighed, louder than she intended.

"Oh, my. What are you *doing* up here? You were just in the living room a minute ago . . . We got to talking about your writing and the movie—I wanted to show off your Hollinger."

With a fake flourish, Quinn pointed toward the award on her shelf, a copper sculpture of a spiral stack of books.

There it is. Are you done here now?

The procession of hugs, pat-pats, and apologies from the sheepish group started immediately. Leigh was the last.

"Come downstairs. Please," she said, holding Quinn's

arms at the elbows. More widow code: *I'm trying hard to help you, but you're not cooperating.*

"In a minute. I need to freshen up."

Freshen up, who said that anymore?

Someone who wished she would go downstairs and find that everyone in her house had magically vanished, that's who.

In the bathroom, she splashed a few handfuls of cold water on her cheeks, careful not to wet her mascara, the first makeup she had put on in over a year. It wasn't her idea. When Leigh arrived earlier, she suggested Quinn apply some—"at least lipstick and mascara—you'll feel so much better."

Right. As if a swish of lip color and thicker lashes would fill the hollowness. But she did it, to show Leigh she was trying. Trying for what, though, she wasn't sure.

This time when she descended the back stairway, his voice stopped her as she reached the breakfast nook off the kitchen. She stood still to listen.

He was talking to the caterers. Of course he was—on his show, he was the guy who tagged along with chefs and home cooks to the local market, wherever local was in that episode—and later joined them in their kitchen to chop and cook and talk about the food.

When she was adapting *Market Day* into the screenplay, Leigh had suggested bringing him on board to get the details of the market scenes just right. The team thought it was a great idea, and since he and Leigh were longtime friends, he had eagerly agreed to help.

The talking stopped, and he came to stand beside her at the dark octagonal windows by the table for two she no longer used. Another reminder, another empty place.

The amber beer bottle and wet blue napkin were still in

his hand. Before, she would have offered him a fresh drink and a new napkin that didn't stain his fingers. Now? Who cared about being polite.

"Hey. I thought I saw you come down." His voice was deep and resonant; she felt it as much as she heard it. He nodded toward the steps. "How are you holding up, considering you have people traipsing all over your house?" Maybe he had noticed the tour group earlier. "Do you even know everyone?" he asked.

"Most. The rest, no idea."

His laugh came out as a huff. "I'm not sure what she was thinking." He was quiet for a beat, then added, "I'm sorry."

"You know Leigh."

"I do. She tries, but sometimes she hits the wrong note."

Now she was the one to make the huffing sound. "That's a kind way to put it."

Dishes and silverware clinked and clattered behind them in the kitchen, the sounds underlaid by faint notes of a saxophone, but the two of them were quiet.

She used to be good at making conversation, at finding questions to ask to learn about people, but that too had vanished. Instead, she tried to focus on the May breeze coming in through the screen, a mix of salty sea air and cigarette smoke from the drivers. The scent of mint and leather, though, that wasn't coming from outside.

She closed her eyes and inhaled again. No, definitely not from outside.

His voice broke their silence. "When I said I was sorry . . . I meant not only about Leigh's overenthusiasm; I meant all of it. What happened. I am, truly, sorry."

She nodded. "I know. Me, too."

"If Leigh heard me say this to you, she would tell me I

was being rude, but . . . All those things people say? They're bullshit. It didn't happen for a reason. It wasn't his time. And no matter how hard anyone tries, not a single one of us here tonight knows what you're going through. People don't know what to do with someone else's grief. It's such a personal, private thing."

He didn't so much as glance toward her while he spoke, respecting her isolation. And although not the most profound, his words were the most understanding ones anyone had spoken to her since that day.

The muscles around her jaw loosened, and the tension that had compressed her body from all directions relaxed the tiniest bit.

The surprising sense of ease muted the thank you she had been about to say. Instead, she turned toward him, looked up at his face, and followed his gaze. It led her beyond the driveway, past the dune grass, toward the swath of dark ocean. Like his kind eyes, the sea glittered in the distance, reflecting the nearly full moon.

They stood still, continuing to look out toward the beach, the water. The fresh air, the sea, the earthy-leathery mint—the scents mingled and soothed, and she inhaled deeply.

Soon, low voices coming from the driveway broke their quiet. Car doors closed in succession. An engine revved to life. Thank goodness; guests were leaving. "I should probably go say goodbye," she told him.

As she turned to leave, her shoulder brushed his upper arm. Warmth radiated through the fabric of his blue button-down shirt. She hadn't realized they were standing this close.

She paused for the briefest moment, startled by the

contact and even more surprised by the unexpected and overpowering craving for more.

———

HE WATCHED her turn and walk through the enormous kitchen, past the busy catering staff. Some of the men glanced up from the leftovers they were wrapping to look at her. He had seen similar reactions when they were on set. Then, like now, she seemed oblivious to it.

Maybe that was one of the reasons it was so hard not to look at her. Loose waves of dark brown hair that, in the California sunlight, had taken on sheens of burgundy. Chocolate-brown eyes alive with interest and curiosity.

He hoped what he said just now wasn't out of bounds. They really didn't know each other well—they had spent a few long, chaotic days working together with the director and actors, and he had liked her at once.

Not liked-her, liked-her—at the time he was entangled in his own drama, and she was happily married to the judge.

Harris had flown to L.A. and come to the set, on a brief break from a big case but said he just needed to see her. It was a surprise; he arrived with a bouquet of flowers, and she broke into a smile Jonathan would never forget.

She ran to Harris and held the back of his neck when they kissed. Everyone made silly cooing sounds and, the next morning, teased her about why the two of them had not emerged from her hotel room for dinner.

Still, you couldn't ignore her poise and contentment, how easily she laughed. She was so different from some of the arrogant personalities Jonathan knew, without a whiff of conceit or self-absorption. Even when the director would challenge everyone's patience at the end of a fourteen-hour day, the volume and tone of her voice stayed even, calm.

Jonathan had read all of her books long before Leigh had asked him to consult—he knew she was creative and smart. When she shared her ideas, you gave her your full attention.

But now . . . now she looked like a ghost, a shell, so different from that vivacious woman. Leigh shocked him when she called a year or so ago to tell him what happened.

He wouldn't wish a tragedy like that on his worst enemy.

He leaned back against the windowsill and took a swig of beer from the bottle he'd been nursing all evening. The smell of cigarette smoke from outside drifted into his nostrils and set him jonesing. He quit years ago at Delphine's request, but with no wife around to stop him now, he would bum one from Gil when he got to the car.

One by one, the catering staff filed out and in, still bringing plates and glasses and chafing dishes in from the living room, the party—or whatever it was—now winding down.

He wondered how Leigh had convinced Quinn to go for this. She had tried to escape more than once tonight; she could not have been comfortable with it. He thought back. The invitation had come from Leigh, a voice mail. Small dinner; nothing fancy; it will be good for Quinn.

And that was why he had come, to help in some way, however small. She was a good person and he didn't know what else he could possibly do.

He said goodnight to the kitchen crew as he went into the living room. The crowd had thinned. The guests who remained were air-kissing and making plans they probably wouldn't keep. He walked among the disbanding groups looking for her to say goodbye, but it was like she had disappeared again.

On his third round, he spotted her coming from the kitchen. She stopped and leaned against the archway to the living room to adjust her shoe and whisk a strand of hair off her face.

Maybe she had gone outside for air. Maybe she too was jonesing for a smoke. Not that he remembered her smoking when they were in L.A.

Before he reached her, a couple he didn't recognize approached, the woman's arms out to hug her. Leigh and a few others gathered near him to wait.

"Well, that was a success." Leigh's short silver hair bounced in satisfaction as she turned from watching Quinn with her piercing blue eyes to face him.

"You outdid yourself. But she looks tired; I think she might need some space."

"She's had nothing but space for the last year—this was good for her. She needs to get back to some semblance of normal."

He was glad Leigh was whispering and that Quinn was busy with the couple so she couldn't hear this.

But before he could answer, the couple walked away, and Leigh stepped forward, hugged Quinn, and pulled back. "See? That wasn't so bad, was it?"

Quinn forced a smile. Nothing above the tip of her nose budged.

She opened her mouth, presumably to respond, but Leigh's question must have been rhetorical because she kept right on going. "Do you have a few minutes to talk after everyone leaves? We should get that proposal to Nely this week."

Nely. Nely Mayano, head of an imprint at Devon, Quinn's publisher. *Man, Leigh, give her a break.*

"I know." Quinn rolled her lips in on themselves like she was holding back. "Let's talk about it tomorrow. It's late. You've already done a lot. Come on, I'll walk you out."

"That's okay, finish saying goodnight." Leigh gestured to the queue that had formed. "You forget—I know this place like the back of my hand."

He doubted Quinn forgot after how Leigh had led that little house tour for the rubberneckers.

When the last pair left, he went to her. "I'm going to take off, too. Look, um . . ."

He planned to tell her if she needed anything to please call him, but how many men had said that to her with different intentions since it happened?

How many men had said that to her tonight?

"I hope what I said earlier didn't upset you."

She shook her head efficiently, once to each side.

"Okay, good." He stuck his hands in his pockets and felt his shoulders shrug. What could he offer that wasn't one more inadequate cliché?

As he stumbled to speak, she drew close and tipped up on her toes as if she wanted to tell him a secret. She took hold of his elbows for balance, each thumb molding perfectly into the crook, the pressure of her fingers warm on the back of his arms.

His ear tingled as she whispered, "I sent your driver away."

2

FEVERISH DANCERS

A few straggling guests chatted by the front door and she ushered them out, locking the door behind them. He followed her to the kitchen, and his cock stirred when she told the catering crew they could leave. "It's late. I'll finish up tomorrow. Really, it's fine. Thank you so much."

The back entrance opened and closed, and then they were alone.

She went to the living room, paused, and crossed her arms as she turned back toward him. "Drink?"

He cleared his throat. He needed something. "Gin and tonic?" Neat would be better, but he wasn't sure what she had in mind. Best to keep his head clear.

She nodded and strode to the carved antique wooden bar against the wall, the only old piece of furniture in the room. It fit, though. The house was contemporary and eclectic, comfortable in that casual, beachy style.

There was no mistaking the owners had money, but they didn't flaunt it. Harris was a highly respected attorney, appointed a judge some time before the movie. And Quinn, well, she was Quinn Layborn, and she had sold millions of books.

At the bar, she turned over two tumblers, popped the cork stopper from the squat black bottle of gin, and poured.

The slender bottle of boutique tonic water hissed as she twisted off the cap, and she emptied it into one of the glasses. She picked up the other tumbler and took one long swallow, closing her eyes as it went down. She refilled it, then picked up both drinks, and came toward him, her stride graceful and deliberate.

"Thanks." His voice cracked like a teenager's when she handed him the tumbler.

"There's no more ice."

He looked down at the clear liquid he couldn't wait to get into his body. "I didn't notice."

"And I forgot the lime." It was a dead-end statement, not like she was telling him she was about to go grab a wedge from the refrigerator.

He shook his head. His mouth was totally bone-dry. Nope, didn't notice that either. "Don't worry, it's fine."

She lifted her glass to her lips, emptied the contents again in one swallow, and set it down on a side table. He took a long swig and set his down too. He would not waste valuable time drinking when she was looking at him with those doe eyes and reaching her hand toward his arm.

Her fingers grazed the skin of his wrist, and he grew hard as they closed around it. A sign of things to come? He hoped like bloody hell, but did not dare assume.

I sent your driver away. What else could that mean?

She led him toward the main staircase, pausing briefly at a panel on the wall to turn off the lights. The house grew dark, and the background hum he hadn't noticed until this moment faded to nothing, amplifying the pulse in his ears and the sound of her heels against the wood floor.

With each step, her hips swayed and the hemline of her black dress rode higher up her thigh. He paused on the landing. Two steps above him, she stopped and looked back.

"Shouldn't I go?" He said a silent prayer. *Please say no.*

"If you want to." Moonlight through the tall glass panels on either side of the front door softly lit half her face. The shadows cast by the grilles created the illusion she stood behind bars, while the rest of her body remained silhouetted in darkness. "But I'd like you to stay."

He felt himself nod. This was surreal. "Of course I will."

Now his cock focused fully. It was no longer holding back, keeping hope in check in case she agreed he should leave.

She was lovely, and she was leading him by the arm to, given his best guess and fervent hope, fuck.

A long time had passed since his last one-night stand. After the public spectacle with Delphine, he promised himself he wouldn't get involved with anyone, on any level, until he was sure he wouldn't screw it up.

He might have destroyed his marriage, but he was not stupid enough to turn down the woman standing before him. The one he had felt oddly protective of all evening as he watched her struggle to feign normalcy.

He reached out to put his hands on her hips, to rub his thumbs along the silky fabric covering her curves, but stopped himself. She should lead; she would show him what she wanted. Grief was an unrelenting bastard. If she needed someone to fuck tonight to get out from under it for a little while—and for whatever reason, he was the lucky son of a bitch she picked—he would give her whatever she was after.

At the top of the stairs, she led him to a bedroom.

The light through the windows and the nightlight in the hall cast enough glow for him to make out the contours of the bed and two nightstands. Near the window was a chaise lounge, several stacks of books beside it on the floor.

They stood facing each other as her breath rustled the hairs near his collar, sending a shot of arousal straight to his dick. She flattened her hands on his chest, her gaze fixed there.

Was he the first since her husband? He guessed yes. Maybe he should ask.

She closed her eyes and began to unbutton his shirt, tugging it from his pants. On the other hand, maybe he should skip the questions.

He bent his head and moved closer to kiss her, and she tilted her head up toward him but turned away without letting her parted mouth meet his. She undid his belt buckle, unfastened the button of his slacks, and lowered the zipper.

Her breathing grew louder as she traced the outline of his cock through the front of his boxers. He wondered if she noticed it twitch.

She reached behind her and unclasped her necklace, two intertwining silver, or more likely platinum, hearts with a diamond set off-center between them.

Carefully, she placed it on the night table and then reached back again for the zipper of her dress.

"Here," he said, slowly turning her around by her raised elbows, "may I?"

He unzipped the dress, and she wiggled it down to the floor, stepped out of it one shiny black high-heeled pump after the other. He could tell by the economy of her movements, she had no clue how sexy she looked as she unhooked her black bra and tossed it on the floor near the closet, then did the same with her black lace panties.

She stood naked in front of him. His breathing caught. So that's where the phrase came from—*breathtaking*.

"You're beautiful," he whispered.

She covered his mouth with her index finger—*be quiet*— then reached into his boxers and put her hand around the underside of him, moving once, twice, up and down the shaft, feeling the head with the pads of her fingers and letting go of him only long enough for him to squirm out of his remaining clothes.

He stood still while she worked him, alternately watching her and looking away. If he focused too hard on what she was doing, it would be over in a heartbeat.

Silently, he counted backward.

100, 99, 98 . . .

He looked down just as she stroked his glans with the side of her thumb. She was going to require a whole different scale.

1000, 999, 998 . . .

Probably sensing he was dangerously close, she let go of him and studied the floor, like she wasn't sure what to do next. He reached his hand to lift her chin with his finger, but again she turned away. Not sharply, but enough to make it clear she didn't want his tenderness.

He waited. He could go slow. Slow was okay.

Actually, slow was good. *997 . . .*

She took a few steps toward the bed and climbed onto it. He followed her in silence, not daring to say anything. And then she got on all fours and shifted her ass back toward him.

973, 972, 971 . . .

He knelt in back of her, circling his hands over the smooth skin of her hips. With each pass, he widened the terrain of her body that he touched until he was caressing the globes of her ass and her thighs. Moist heat radiated from between them.

892 . . .

With one hand, he reached between her parted legs and stroked her, dragging his finger along her slippery folds. If her wetness didn't tell him she was ready for him, the moan she let out, and the drop of her head in relief, did.

But maybe she didn't want him inside her so soon. He felt stupid inquiring; he had slept with plenty of women. Here was someone he barely knew unexpectedly giving herself over to him. It was not the time to ask for directions.

He touched her some more, making tiny circles around her swollen bead, moving along her lips, sliding one finger, then two, inside her. He tried to tune out the noises of pleasure she made as he moved steadily in her velvet heat.

Only it was a lost cause, impossible not to watch her, impossible not to bask in those sounds.

He was adrift hell-knows-where in the 500s when she reached back for him. With her soft, warm hand around his shaft, she guided him toward her entrance.

Shit! Condom. For the love of everything holy, please. Please. Wallet.

He patted her ass. "Give me a second; I hope I have a condom," he whispered. "You don't . . . ?"

Her head dropped again as she sighed. Of course she didn't have a rubber laying around. "I can't get pregnant, and you won't catch anything."

"I'm not worried about me." He trusted she was clean,

and he had been tested. Even so, she shouldn't put herself at risk—with him or anyone else.

"It's fine—I don't care."

Whoa. "It's not fine. You need to protect yourself."

She turned and glared. "Don't lecture me."

The mood was rapidly evaporating. "You're right, I'm sorry. I'm going to check."

He touched her low back gently to reinforce his apology before locating the billfold in the heap of gray cloth that was his pants on her bedroom floor.

The innermost compartment—yes!—he may have sworn off dating but at least he hadn't cleaned out his wallet.

He tore open the package and slid the rubber on. Even their tense exchange did not dampen his enthusiasm.

As he approached, he caressed her hips again, circling her ass, teasing her inner thighs, returning to her pussy, just as wet as when he walked away a moment ago.

She shifted her hips backward in his direction once more and he entered her slowly, giving her a chance to expand around him. Past encounters had taught him not to rush. He wasn't likely to be cast in any porn flicks, but he wasn't small either. She surprised him with a cry and thrust backward to take him in.

468. 467.

His balls slapped against her as their speed increased.

502 . . . 242?

She lowered her shoulders and head to the bed and used a now-free hand to rub herself in small, circular motions. She moaned, and he held fast to her hips, penetrating her even deeper.

It was delicious. She was delicious. Hot and wet and tight and . . . 821 . . .

But it was too late. Watching her, feeling her, it sent him over the edge.

"I'm there," he warned.

And so was she.

Her breath hitched, a little gasp, and she squeezed around him rhythmically as though drawing the climax out of him, contraction by glorious contraction.

After, they lay quietly as her breathing returned to a normal pace, she on her belly, the tops of her feet dangling over the edge of the bed, her forehead resting on her hands, while he turned onto his back, leaving an arm's length between them.

He resisted the urge to touch her while he considered what to say. He didn't want to think about her with other men given what they had just done, but he wanted to talk about her condom comment, about not caring.

If he remembered right, she was a couple of years younger than his forty-eight years; she had a long sex life ahead of her.

But then he remembered how she held her finger to his lips earlier, asking him not to speak.

He would find another way to address it. If he learned anything in the last hour, it was how words were only one of many ways to communicate.

What she did shortly after certainly conveyed the message.

She turned over and drew her legs up so her knees were bent, then slid two fingers into her pussy. Her lack of inhibition with him, her hunger and urgency, they surprised and aroused him, aroused being a woeful understatement.

Watching her fingers glisten with her wetness each time she withdrew them—if he didn't just come, he would have gotten hard in record time.

Her back and neck arched, her movements sensual but uncontrived, making her seem present in a way she wasn't all night.

Please, allow me.

He got up from the bed and knelt in front of her. He watched up close as her fingers moved, the sounds causing him to wish he could direct enough blood to his cock for a second go. But he wasn't a spring chicken; he needed a bit more time.

Instead, he pressed his thumb against her clit and circled. Using his other hand, he inserted his finger with hers. She moaned as her head tipped farther back as they pleasured her together.

He turned his hand so he could feel his way along her walls to that pad of sensitive flesh, stroking it with light but consistent pressure.

She whimpered in time with his movements until the individual sounds came together in a long moan.

Her hips bucked off the bed and she cried out, but he stayed with her, continuing the pressure and the motion, stroke after stroke after stroke as she squeezed and released again and again around their fingers.

He tried to take hold of her free hand, to hold it while she came, but she moved it away.

Understood.

Afterward, they lay on their backs, two parallel lines. He turned his head so he could see her. "You okay?"

As she nodded, the waves of her hair brushed against the pillowcase. That was enough; he wouldn't press. They had been intimate but only exchanged, what, ten words?

They must have dozed. As soon as he opened his eyes and looked at her, she took hold of him again.

Her hand felt so good around him. She sat up, sliding it

up and down his length. And then she moved to straddle him.

It occurred to him that maybe he was still asleep and this was all a dream. A frigging wet and fantastic dream.

His thumbs caressed her hips.

She held the base of his cock and lowered herself onto him with a moan. Nope, not a dream. *999, 998 ...*

SHE WAS full with him inside her, consumed with something beside the weight of desolation. It had become less paralyzing as the months wore on, but still it was always there, a thick fog that shrouded her, blurred her view, locked her in.

She and Harris were married for eighteen years, knew each other for more than twenty. Would learning to live without him mirror the time their lives were woven together? Would it take another two decades to stop missing him from deep in her bones?

How was she supposed to piece herself back together after such a large part of her life was gone?

She had never cheated. Not only because of the marriage vows they exchanged or their mutual promises to be faithful, but because she had been happy. She had no desire to sleep with anyone else.

But now, it felt like cheating, with another man's hands on her hips, guiding her less-than-graceful forays along his cock.

Desire had hit her so hard tonight, a jarring blow to the gut. Maybe it was all the men, with their deep voices, their warmth, their masculinity, their life.

She would catch the scent of cologne, a glimpse of chest

hair at the notch of a dress shirt, feel the rasp of five o'clock shadow across her cheek as they said hello and goodbye, and she had, inexplicably, felt herself heat from within, swollen and damp.

But a lot of the men had wives, and many of them had had ties to Harris.

Jonathan had neither. Better yet, he had a reputation.

The commitment-phobe who would have no illusions about this being any kind of relationship, who would no doubt be discreet after his scandal a couple of years ago.

She didn't need to be the subject of gossip. You could be damn sure the same women who pat-patted her back tonight and urged her to get out more would be the first to whisper and tsk about how inappropriate it would be for the grieving widow to fuck someone else.

He was gone barely over a year. Can you believe it? Already, she has a boyfriend.

But let them live in her shoes. Let them lose what she lost. Then let them talk about appropriate.

What she did now shouldn't matter to anyone—nothing really mattered even to her now—but still, who she fucked and when was her business.

But it wasn't only discretion. Jonathan's height and broad shoulders that narrowed toward his waist, the way his gray slacks fell over his ass, were extremely sexy. She didn't remember him being so handsome on the set, but maybe she wasn't paying attention.

But the most compelling things about him, the things that sent her outside to ask which of the remaining drivers had brought him, were the understanding in his eyes and the simple, blunt way he spoke to her in the kitchen.

He had not expected anything from her in response. He had not so much as looked at her when he spoke. He knew how to be with her and leave her alone at the same time. Gifts.

His words and, ironically, his distance, drove her to act, to turn the craving for a man's body against hers tonight into reality.

Just this once.

And now his large hands were holding tight to her hips as she continued to ride him. His hair tickled her lips each time she came down on him. Her pussy was sore, each entry and withdrawal amplifying the burn and the sting and the ache.

To drown out the guilt, she focused hard on the pain, letting it converge with sensation instead. The throb made her movements faster, more furious, the burn spreading along her lips and inside her passage, tight with his thickness.

The heat and the pain swirled, feverish dancers winding into something else.

Sugar spinning into candy, ache whirling into oblivion. This is what she needed; this is what she had chosen him for.

Her fingertips heated when she pressed into the hot skin of his belly as she reached the brink of exploding, involuntarily squeezing around him over and over and over.

When she caught her breath, she climbed off him and sat near his waist. She put a hand around him to finish him off. Only a few strokes and he grunted, cum spurting, dripping over her thumb and onto the sheet.

She moved away from him and laid back on the bed, their bodies far enough apart so he couldn't easily reach her. She glanced at the clock.

It was late. She wouldn't ask him to leave at this hour, but she did not want to be held. Chilled from a dewy layer of sweat, she pulled the bunched sheet up from the foot of the bed over them. Maybe now she could finally sleep.

She could not. She got out of bed, grabbed her robe from the chaise, wrapped it around herself, and went to the bathroom, closing the door softly.

The cool night air inched in as she opened the window and sat on the wide ledge of the tub. He had not disappointed. He was attentive and responsive and quiet. With him, she could be somewhere else.

When they were on the movie set three years ago, he was different, brash with the producers, the actors, the director. To her, he lobbed question after question about her novel and characters, their motivations, how she envisioned the story. She appreciated his enthusiasm, but he also had come across as a tad full of himself. Not that she cared as long as he did his work.

A while after they worked together, Quinn heard snippets here and there about him: cheating, divorce, fall from grace, brought down a peg or two. There was even some embarrassing hashtag on social media, if she remembered correctly. But maybe she didn't; that old life was forever ago.

The porcelain ledge of the tub was cold against the back of her thighs. She planned to take a bath, wash away the stickiness and the sweat and the scent, and be by herself in here a while longer.

Instead, she stood and started toward the door; no, she wouldn't wash, not yet. The drying fluids pulling her skin taut, the dank smell of cum, they were a reminder that, least of all, she was guilty of fucking a man she barely knew.

She undressed in front of him. Although she avoided looking at him at first, she fucked him several times, deliberately and hungrily. And still, she wanted more. What kind of wife did that make her?

What kind of widow?

The tears fell down her cheeks as she left the bathroom, tip-toed across the room and slid back into bed, turning away from the foreign body sleeping beside her.

It was just this once.

When she woke to the early light outside, he wasn't in the bed. She closed her eyes again. If he were waiting for her downstairs, sitting on the couch or at the kitchen table reading something on his phone, maybe he would give up and leave.

As alone as she felt the past year, still she craved isolation. Even while he was inside her last night.

That's how it had been, with the friends who came to visit, with the people who pressured her to go out for dinner or take a walk or attend some fundraising event she felt too bad to say no to, she was by herself.

When her longtime writers' group begged her to come back, just to sit and listen and be back among them, she had sat there like a zombie, unable to absorb the words, the stories being spoken around her.

During their wine break, she told a colleague she was going to the bathroom but instead snuck out the door, ignored their calls, and had not gone back since.

When it seemed like enough time passed without noise from the lower level, she got up, re-tied her robe, and went down the back stairs to the kitchen.

On the center island sat a plate with an omelette—brie and mushrooms, items she never would have had if the caterers didn't wrap up last night's leftovers.

A sliced strawberry fanned out on the edge, and a sprinkling of chives dusted the rest of the plate. Gleaming silverware that wasn't hers lay on a folded cloth napkin. A glass of orange juice sat nearby, covered tightly with plastic wrap.

For some reason, he chose to protect the juice but not the food, as if one were more vulnerable than the other. She didn't know why she thought about it so hard as she picked at the breakfast he prepared. She could ask if she were to see him again, but she would not.

3

HIDDEN CAMERA REALITY SHOW?

H e leaned against the leather headrest and caught Gil's sidelong glance in the rearview mirror. "Everything okay, Mr. Jaines?"

His exhale stifled a dry laugh. "Yeah, everything's fine." He had known Gil since the network hired him for the show years ago, and no matter how many times he asked Gil to call him Jonathan, the man refused to use his first name.

"Back to the city?"

"Back to the city."

He closed his eyes and pictured Quinn coming downstairs, pleased he hoped, with the breakfast he left, although it was less about the food and more that he couldn't think of what else to do.

It was close to three a.m. when they finally lay back on the pillows, exhausted. In the blur of restless sleep that followed, he heard her toss and turn, get out of bed and, at some point, sniff as if she might be crying.

He wanted to reach out and touch her back, pull her

closer. But he knew enough from the previous few hours to realize she wouldn't want that, so he let her be.

When he woke up around six, her body was rising and falling steadily and he didn't want to wake her. At first he had gone to the kitchen looking for a junk drawer with a pencil and paper so he could leave a note. But what would he write? Had a great time? Call me?

Seriously, had it been some hidden camera reality show? Maybe a ruse to make a porno?

Or she was going to try to blackmail him with a sex tape. Jesus. It was just like porn, only better. She was beautiful. Her pussy was beautiful. Her breasts were beautiful. She clenched the entire length of him and took charge of her own pleasure, making it clear to him what she wanted.

It was much better than porn—it was real, primal. Leaving a note on her kitchen counter would have been shitty; it would ruin whatever magical sex world had cocooned the two of them last night.

He had scanned the gigantic kitchen for other ideas, noting a clay pot of chives next to a pair of scissors on the counter. He could make her breakfast, a nice omelette maybe, garnish it with chives. Who could argue with an omelette?

In the fridge, he found mushrooms from last night's veggie tray and a wedge of nice brie from one of the cheese boards. Quietly, he got to work locating a whisk and cooking the eggs.

When it was ready, he set her a place at the granite island facing the window and left the washed pan, cutting board, and utensils in the drying rack by the farmhouse sink.

He wiped his hands on a dishtowel and looked around again. Her kitchen was incredible—the big stone island, a butler's pantry with a second set of appliances, the octagonal breakfast nook where he stood with her last night at the windows, looking out over the property and the ocean.

It was a great place, their house. Her house now. His heart hurt for her. The weathered cedar siding, the comfortable, classy furniture, the breezy eastern Long Island waterfront estate—none of it would ease the pain of that loss.

While he made her breakfast, he noticed a low hedge with big round pink flowers—he had no clue what kind they were—bordering a garden path. He contemplated going out to cut one to put in a glass near her plate, but that seemed too romantic and he guessed she would find it sappy if not intrusive.

There were some scrap pieces of plastic wrap on the counter, and he covered her juice glass with the smallest one. She would probably come down in a minute, before the plate got cold. He pictured her at the top of the stairs, waiting. Listening for him to leave.

He wondered if she would eat at the island or the breakfast nook or perhaps her office. Where did one eat alone in such a big house? After Delphine left, he would stand at the kitchen island and scarf his food. At least a quiet apartment heckled you with fewer choices.

Maybe Quinn would eat while she wrote. He imagined her drifting through the rooms to her office like a lonely ghost. There but not there.

Last night she had been among so many people but not with them; it was as if she were hiding in plain sight.

After Delphine moved out, he had been a mess, but that was nothing compared with the loss Quinn experienced. For one thing, he brought his divorce on entirely himself, fucking up his marriage beyond all recognition.

For another thing, although she hated his guts, Delphine had not suddenly died and left him alone.

His head fell forward and he jerked awake. They were stop and go in the Midtown Tunnel, which would soon—hopefully sometime today, given the traffic—hock them out like a smoker's cough near his apartment.

He rubbed his eyes with his thumb and forefinger and, when he looked up, caught Gil's glance in the mirror once more.

"What's the rest of the day look like, Mr. Jaines?"

Shit, it was only Thursday. "It looks like a Bloody Mary."

Gil laughed as they got closer to the apartment, and Jonathan pulled out his phone to check his calendar. "I may need to go to the office later; let me catch up on messages and text you once I know what's going on."

Barnes, the building's doorman, greeted Jonathan as he opened the door. With a swipe of his key card near the elevator reader, the bronze art deco gate opened and slid shut a moment after he stepped in.

It opened on the penthouse landing, and he set his keys on the stainless and glass console table in the entry gallery. A lot had happened since he picked them up last night on his way out the door to Quinn's.

As it always did, the abstract painting that hung above the table drew his eye straight to the raised scar near the lower left corner.

Universe, it was called. He and Delphine had seen it together at a gallery show. Something about it spoke to him, its colors and depth, and he returned to look at it several times that night.

Each time he had stood in a different spot—closer to it,

further, off to the left or to the right, trying to read its visual message from multiple angles.

A couple of weeks later, when he came home from shooting an episode in Dublin—and banging his girlfriend on the way back—the canvas was hanging here, a touching, loving surprise.

A few days after that, his phone vibrated later in the evening than usual. It could have been anyone, but when he declined the call, Delphine flat-out asked. "Are you having an affair?"

What did it say about him that this had stunned him?

"Of course not."

But then she showed him her phone, with a blurry but no less damning photo of Anna and him coming out of a private shower room in the airport's first-class lounge, on its screen.

He didn't remember now what pathetic shit he said in response, probably something like, "It's not what it looks like."

Although that was exactly what it was.

He had met Anna during a layover, pun not intended, on a prior trip. They flirted by text, then sext, and coordinated flights and cities to meet again.

The affair continued in that vein, a series of trysts in cities they both passed through on the way to somewhere else.

It was so appallingly cliché, including the part where some asshole at the airport recognized him, sold a couple of pictures to a tabloid, and posted all over social media.

He still wished he could have a do-over, turn back the clock and handle the situation like a better man.

He and Delphine barely spoke after that night. Divorce

papers were served, angry meetings took place in attorneys' offices, and then their relationship went dark.

Shame had dogged him since. Not only because of the affair itself but because of how he lied. He had been so ashamed, he had not been able to talk about it with her.

That night—the Night of Getting Real, he called it— after more of his denials, she smacked him across the face, hard.

He could still hear the sound and feel the sting on his cheek. More than the physical force, the sudden realization of the meaning and impact of his lies, his betrayal, and of the depth of her hurt and anger knocked him off balance, causing him to lose his footing and stumble backward.

He never in his life felt as small, as sorry, as full of regret and self-loathing as he did in that moment.

How had he not understood all of this before? But by then it was too late.

She stormed into the bedroom and came out quickly, pulling a small suitcase—too quickly for his false denials to have surprised her.

On her way to the elevator, she raised her hand to the painting and slashed it with the point of the diamond in her engagement ring.

Then she turned to him and in an eerily calm voice called him a fucking, lying prick.

A fuc-king, ly-ing prick.

He wished she had screamed so he could tell himself she was overreacting, or that she called him something else, something less rhythmic.

Because the cadence of that phrase echoed his own thoughts and tunneled its way through his eardrums and into his brain, lodging itself in some remote cluster of cells no amount of booze or weed or sessions with a shrink had yet been able to quell.

The sound of her smacking his face earlier, that lodged there too, reminding him how badly he treated her, how much he deserved her wrath. Reminding him he had been a coward and a liar.

He got the painting repaired. If you didn't know there had been a gash, your eye would move right past it. But he forced himself to look at its scar, the tight ridge of canvas, each time he walked past it so he would not forget what he had mindlessly done for reasons he still could not fully identify.

And so he would not repeat it.

Today, sound burbled from the living room TV he left on yesterday. He picked up the remote and turned the volume higher until noise filled the room. He still hated coming home to the silence.

With the TV eating up electricity twenty-four seven, he was probably Con Edison's best customer.

In the bedroom, he contemplated a quick nap but settled on a shower to clear his head. His limp dick twitched to life as his boxers brushed against it when he took them off.

He imagined the fabric was Quinn's hand, reaching for him, guiding him into her. There was baby oil under the sink, and he poured some into his palm, pretending it was her juice and his jerking hand, her body pulsing around him.

She would not have fucked him like that if she saw him now, jacking off like a teenager as he stepped into the cavernous shower-for-two, tugging at his full sac before aiming the spurting release toward the drain.

SHE STARED out the window of her office and tried to think about something other than him, when her phone buzzed on the desk.

Hitting "ignore" again wasn't an option.

She already avoided several calls this morning, which was nothing compared to how many she ignored the past year.

But it was Leigh. Leigh, who had her best interests at heart. Leigh, who had guided her career to a level of success she might not have reached otherwise. Eleven best-selling novels, foreign rights all over the world, and a film deal that brought *Market Day* to life.

Leigh, whose usual lively voice was subdued today. Quinn knew her—she was going to tiptoe toward the real reason for calling.

"Dinner the other night was lovely . . . Hope you got some rest."

And then the predictable shift in tone.

It was impossible to focus on the thread of her words, which were breaking up even though the connection was fine. "Nely called again this morning . . . asked about the book. When can they expect to see the chapter outline . . . some pages? . . . I told her it's been a rough road. This was a terrible month . . . the anniversary a few weeks ago . . . I'm supposed to check in with you . . . update on progress."

Leigh paused. "I need to relay *something*, so I have to ask . . ."

Quinn sighed.

Leigh's tiptoe voice again: "I know how hard it's been."

Do you? How do you know how hard it's been?

She heard Jonathan's deep voice echo in her mind. *Not a single one of us here tonight knows how you feel.*

He was right. Of all those people, including Leigh, he was the only one sensitive enough not to expect normalcy from her. Whatever normalcy meant now, she had no idea.

"You have to remember . . . purely a business deal for them . . . nothing personal . . . they gave us a deadline extension . . . important to keep momentum going . . . fans engaged . . . How can I help?"

"You can't. I know what I have to do."

It's just that I can't.

". . . such a wonderful writer. If anyone can pull out of this, this funk, this block, it's . . . Get the words down . . . check with you . . . couple of days."

It used to come easy, the writing. Well, not easy, but it was the fire in her belly. Awake early, at her desk or walking on the beach at sunrise, dictating into her phone or sitting by the water with a pen and notepad.

She kept a pad by the bed, a notebook in her purse, a notebook in the glove box. The ideas would come, the scenes, character quirks, a line of dialogue, ideas for how to go deeper into a theme.

Oh, there would be snags with a plot or a character, exhausting book tours and repetitive talks, critical reviews she could not let go of no matter how many positive ones came before or after or how many copies sold.

But writing was her career, her creative outlet, her hobby, her love all rolled into one. The stories and words in her mind had flowed, and she often found herself in a place where time dissolved.

She would never forgive herself for letting that love take her away from Harris in his last days.

Leigh was right to prod. That was her job as her agent.

Quinn should try harder. She should try to change her mindset, think about it as delivering a product rather than a piece of her soul.

But as a friend, well, maybe Leigh could aim for a bit more understanding and slightly less prodding.

Over the top of her laptop screen, out the window, the late-day sun seared its reflection on the water. When she at last let herself look away, flashbulbs burst at the back of her eyes, eclipsing the blank page.

Long after the spots faded, she closed the computer and got up to pee. Her lips still burned from last night, like the blinding angle of the sun, fierce and exquisite.

It was just once.

But the sting was impossible to stop thinking about.

She returned to her desk and tapped Leigh's number from the recent calls list. What she was about to say technically wasn't a lie.

"Hi again, sorry to call late. I could use a bit of inspiration. Seeing Jonathan the other night reminded me how helpful he was when we did the movie. I thought I might bounce some ideas off him. Can I have his number?"

4

NO TALKING, NO KISSING

It was a miracle he had gotten anything accomplished the past two days. When he wasn't under pressure to write the week's three behind-the-scenes blog posts, review edits, voice over the promo spots for two upcoming shows, and start researching the lineup and itineraries for next season, his brain went to her.

He could call her now that the day was winding down, if he knew how to reach her.

Her phone had been charging on the kitchen counter when he left, and he was tempted to take her number or enter his so he wouldn't have to ask Leigh. But that was creepy, to go into someone's phone.

And what if she had no intention of a repeat?

Besides, what would he say if he called? Sending a text would be easier, but even that content eluded him.

Rich, the show's production manager, stuck his head around the doorframe of Jonathan's office.

"Dude, we're heading to Susana's Cantina for happy hour. You coming?"

He hesitated for a moment, hoping for some divine telepathic intervention, but nothing came. "You bet. Just finishing up here. I'll catch up."

He bookmarked the browser tabs he had opened, shut down his computer, and checked his phone for the hundredth futile time.

When he got to the restaurant, his team was seated at a table outside. Sirens wailed a few blocks away while a bus released its brake with a blast of air and pulled away from the nearby curb. This was good, the people and the noise and the hustle and, soon, a salt-rimmed shot of tequila.

". . . drink, sir?" The waitress was looking at him impatiently, wanting his order. Good, she didn't recognize him, some middle-aged jerk wearing sunglasses on a cloudy day.

As the evening wore on, the noise level climbed and the age of the crowd fell.

Music drifted out from the band playing inside. They ordered more food. He liked going out with his staff despite the age difference—he had at least a decade, probably closer to two, on most of them. And since he always picked up the tab, they liked going out with him.

They were bright, funny, and hardworking, some of them aspiring to be like him some day. He should tell them not to work *too* hard.

He didn't get this gig because he deserved it; he got it because—okay, maybe he had some skills, but none that truly distinguished him—mostly, he had been plain fucking lucky.

He looked around the table. It hadn't always been like this. Even with his corporate credit card, the team hadn't usually included him in their plans. In the earlier days of the show, he was a dick.

Not because he was any kind of perfectionist, mostly because he thought a dick was how he was supposed to be.

Act like you own it, or it will go away as fast as it landed in your undeserving lap.

And then he met Anna, and somehow cheating on Delphine also seemed like something an insecure, mediocre but lucky travel show host might do to fit the role, so he did.

Might as well play the game, go all in.

His modicum of success had gone to his head. Part of him knew the risks, the irreparable damage if he continued. But he and Anna didn't stop. With each meeting, he swore it would be the last—right until the point he unzipped his pants again.

He would come home and shower. Most of those nights, he slept on the couch. But some, he would get into bed beside Delphine, and she would turn over and want to spoon.

She would say she missed him, and he would say he missed her, too. Which was true—they made great companions. The part he didn't say was that he hadn't thought of her so much while he was having sex with someone else.

They were easy prey for the tabloids, Anna and him, and social media had a field day. He wished he had earned that level of attention from the show. And that the network hadn't had to step in to foot the bill to scrub the negativity, repair the reputation.

He signaled the server as she brought a round of drinks to the next table.

"Make it a double this time, please," he said when she came over.

What he had done to Delphine still disgusted him, and alcohol dulled the sharper edges. He had come perilously close to sinking his career, too.

And that's when the point really hit home that acting

like an entitled douchebag might not be his best strategy for success.

His phone vibrated against the table, and he turned it over. A text message with a 631 area code dropped from the top of the screen like a winning lottery number flashing on the eleven o'clock news.

Are you busy? Can you come?

When the server brought his double, he downed it and handed her his credit card. "You can put it on here when they're done and give the bill to him to sign." He pointed to Rich. Her eyes widened when she saw the name in raised plastic, and she fumbled slipping it into the pocket of her black apron.

"Guys, ladies, I gotta wrap it up," he yelled over the noise. "Have a good time. See you tomorrow."

Luckily, Gil was available to give him a ride—it would be a lot faster than the train—and he texted Quinn as he jogged toward Gil's location, slowing his stride only to duck into a drugstore to buy a pack of rubbers.

On my way.

Traffic was relatively light going in her direction. He pitied the poor assholes sitting bumper to bumper on the other side, creeping their way into Manhattan, still at this hour. With each passing exit off the Long Island Expressway, his dick pressed harder against his jeans.

A COUPLE OF HOURS LATER, he stood outside her house, a house the locals but no one else would call a cottage. Until he landed the show, he had not been around money like this, one more thing that told him he didn't belong, that it was all some big mistake.

She must have been watching the driveway because the door opened as he stepped onto the long, wide front porch.

"Hi," she said as he approached. "I wasn't sure you'd come."

The black silk robe she wore emphasized her sexy body, curvy in all the right places, while the black patent heels made her bare legs appear more alluring than they already were. "Why wouldn't I?"

He bent his head to kiss her cheek, and she turned away, putting her hand on his chest instead. He reminded himself of the unspoken rules—*no talking, no kissing*—and he refrained from asking how she was or explaining how he had wanted to call.

He had played that right—she was not interested in talking.

Instead, she led him inside, through the large foyer and, rather than up the stairs like last time, left into the living room toward the beachy white sectional couch with its deep, overstuffed cushions.

She didn't waste any time unbuttoning his shirt. He pulled his arms out, took it off, and she took it from him to toss onto the coffee table. She unfastened his belt and yanked the button-fly of his jeans apart, then rubbed him through his boxers, wet with pre-cum. He had been hard the whole drive out.

She tugged at the shorts and the waist of his jeans, and he helped her take them off. His cock sprang when he did, while she undid the tie of her robe and let it fall to the floor.

Just like last time, his breath caught at the sight of her.

As they stood face to face, he reached out and touched her neck with the side of his thumb. Her pulse was beating like a hummingbird's.

Bringing her close against him, holding her until she relaxed wasn't an option, so he caressed his way slowly down to her shoulder and then further to her breast. She stood silently for a few moments, her eyes closed as he touched her.

Then, suddenly all business, as if she wanted no more caressing, she went to the arm of the couch, bent over it, stepped her legs apart, and turned to look for him.

Like last time, she would let him know what she wanted.

He retrieved the condom he discreetly put in his jeans pocket during the drive and rolled it on before stepping behind her.

Her ass was at the perfect height and angle, and he ran his hands over the smoothness, using his thumbs to raise the skin and spread her cheeks to look at her. All of her.

She tensed, and he let go. *Note to self: No anal.*

He moved his hand to her hip and with the other reached down and stroked the length of her pussy. Her lips were full and wet already, and he slid a finger inside her, not only for her pleasure, also for his. He had so badly needed to feel her again.

She stepped her feet out a few more inches, spreading wider. Man, he wanted his cock to feel that heat, too.

He withdrew his finger, sucked it clean, positioned his hands around her hips. "Are you ready for me to be inside you?"

"Yes," she answered, and he slid easily into her. Her

upper body relaxed against the soft cushions, as if she were relieved.

He varied his strokes, every so often pulling almost completely out of her, waiting a few seconds until her hips moved in search of him, and then plunging deep and fast.

He paced his movements to hers, the pressure building further as she thrust her hips back toward him.

She reached for a throw pillow and buried her face in it, deeper with each stroke. Her hands kneaded the edge, the fabric muffling her moans. She was close. He sped up, and she thrust back harder. Her cry left him . . . make that both of them . . . shuddering.

He pulled out a few moments later, and slowly she stood.

Light from the driveway lanterns shined through the gaps in the curtains, enough to see her erect nipples, the flush in her cheeks and neck, her lips, darker and more full than he remembered. He stifled the urge to kiss them.

She picked up her robe from the floor, put it on and reached her arm out, leading him—thank you, sweet Jesus— up the stairs and not toward the front door.

She sat on the edge of the bed, in the same room as the other night, and she slid the nightstand drawer open. She pulled out a long silk scarf, handed it to him, and held her wrists out toward him, together.

She wanted him to tie her hands?

Okay, he wouldn't have gone there himself, but he complied, careful not to hurt her by wrapping them too tightly. She lay on her back and brought her bound hands over her head. "Tie them to the bed," she said, quiet but certain.

No, he definitely had not expected this, but he snaked

the long ends of the scarf twice through the headboard and knotted them like she asked.

Sitting back on his haunches, he looked at her, her arms overhead, her gaze distant, and he ran his fingers along the side of her breast and down along her waist. She shivered, and he continued, across her belly, up the center of her torso, over one breast and then the other, her nipples even harder now. He trailed as lightly as possible while still keeping contact with her skin.

When he glanced down, her legs were spread and her hips tipped back and forth, as if an invisible cock—not invisible, make it his—were inside her.

But he wasn't hard enough to take her again yet, so he moved down between her legs, slowly spread her lips with his fingers, listened to her gasp as he touched her, and then tasted her. Delicious. Honey and salt, citrus. Mm. Tangerine.

He explored some more, ran his tongue along her lips, swirled it around her clit. The faster he moved, the more pressure he applied, the more she writhed. He tried teasing and biting her, at first small little nips with his tongue and lips and, as she moaned and wriggled with pleasure, harder with his teeth.

With his mouth still on her, he inserted two fingers. She moaned again and her pussy contracted, pulling them deeper. He worked them like a cock, hard and fast and deep, while he nipped her clit again and again with his teeth and tongue. He slowed for a second to watch her. "Too much?"

She shook her head vigorously, her dark hair sweeping the pillow. *No.*

Her movements told him to go faster, to plunge harder,

but he kept the pressure steady, not wanting her to come before he got inside her.

Fully erect now—*finally*—he slowed and withdrew his fingers. Retrieving another condom, he moved higher on the bed and, although she hadn't asked, he untied the scarf from the headboard. She must have pins and needles by now, with her arms raised like that.

She watched his cock as he sheathed it. With her wrists tied together but her arms free, she got up on her knees and motioned for him to lie down.

When he did, she climbed astride him, closed her eyes, and lowered herself inch by inch all the way down on his pounding dick.

Her bound hands rested on his stomach as she rode him. She would surely be sore later; they had been going at each other hard.

His hands went to her hips. He could not stop touching those hips. With his palm, he traced their curve, slid his hand back and gripped her ass.

"Pull my hair," she said, her voice shaking as she lifted off and sank onto him over and over.

He rubbed her haunches, his thumbs stroking her thighs. "Your hair?"

She nodded and leaned forward, her brown locks falling over her face. He reached for a clump and pulled.

She sighed. "Harder."

He pulled again, holding it a second longer this time.

"*Please*. Harder." There was an anguished edge to her voice, as if she were about to break down and cry.

EXCEPT FOR A COUPLE of limp attempts, he was massaging her scalp. What part of *pull* wasn't clear?

She slowed her pace on his cock, took a deep breath, and sighed in frustration as he wound his fingers through her hair.

But then he yanked, sudden and hard, and a cry flew out from deep in her chest. Her eyes squeezed shut from the sting, and she sped up her movements.

He yanked again, fast and forceful, and her burning scalp and chafed pussy sent a frenzied wave crashing. Her whole body clenched.

She stayed astride him after she came, stretched full, savoring the contractions and the ache.

The pain was her distraction from guilt. The bondage, if you could call it that—he had tied her hands so loosely and tentatively she could easily have slipped out of the knots—kept her from touching him.

All day, each time she succumbed to the urge to think about their previous night together, what she most remembered was how she had wanted to touch him everywhere.

Restraint and pain, they were her distractions from guilt, her punishment for desire, her self-signed permission slip to fuck another man.

But she had not expected their intoxicating effect.

Nothing like this had ever really turned her on before, at least not what she knew of it from the novelty Valentine's Day BDSM kit with its scratchy red scarf, fuzzy handcuffs, and mini riding crop Harris had given her one year.

But now it did turn her on, and she wanted it desperately.

Jonathan seemed to sense her frantic need.

He untied her wrists and she climbed off him. Before she could lie down, though, he caught her arms and guided her down so she sat next to him. Kneeling beside her, he wrapped the cool silk around her hands again.

Only this time, he left no space between her wrists and tied a tight double knot.

She was not slipping out of this one.

He laid her down and again threaded the loose ends of the scarf through the headboard.

He looked down her body, his expression one she couldn't quite read. It was serious and admiring, but there was something in his tightly knit brow.

Maybe now that he'd taken control and bound her in earnest, he was planning what to do next.

Goose bumps rose on her skin.

He got off the bed and walked out of the room, the sound of his footsteps in the hallway moving toward the stairs.

She took a deep breath and exhaled a mix of anxiety and anticipation. She trusted him with her safety, but what if she'd been wrong?

With her hands tied, he could do anything to her.

The thought, and the uncertainty of what would happen when he returned, dissipated into a surprising tingling sensation between her legs.

He came back holding his t-shirt, dropped something else she couldn't see on the floor by the foot of the bed, and sat on the edge.

Holding the shirt horizontally between both hands, he spun it until it narrowed. He laid it over her eyes and guided her onto her side so he could tie it behind the back of her head. He tugged the fabric down further over her eyes until she couldn't see out the bottom.

His fingertips softly touched her upper arm, stretched overhead. "This okay?"

She nodded. *Yes.*

She tracked his movements by sound, by the wisp of his breath grazing her body, by how his weight shifted on the bed. By his radiating heat, by his scent, a trace of plum and leather.

He leaned over her, his breath high on her belly, and brought his mouth to one nipple, the sudden touch of his lips sending a charge through her body.

He did the same with her other breast, just a light touch, as if surveying an unfamiliar landscape. Back to the first, tugging gently, and then not so gently, with his lips and teeth, like he had done earlier with her clit.

He moved between her breasts, pinching one while his mouth lightly tugged and bit the other. Each tweak and nip, a wintertime static shock, an abrupt jolt that ended quickly. Too quickly.

She canted her hips and squeezed her thighs together, a poor attempt to create friction. The more sensation she felt, the more she craved; a need she didn't possess the words to describe hovered just beyond her reach.

He put one hand flat on the lowest stretch of her belly to keep her from writhing. With the other, he separated her legs. She tried to buck against him but he kept her pelvis immobile, teasing her, while he returned his mouth to her nipples. They were sore now when he sucked and twisted, and she breathed in the ache as if it were the air.

The hand he had on her pubic bone slid between her thighs, and he pushed them apart again, less gently this time.

And then he let go of her.

She reached to bring him back, but her arm jerked overhead. *The scarf.*

He left the bed and then his hands were around her

ankles, pulling her down the mattress, stretching her arms straight above her as she slid away from the headboard. He spread her legs wider again and bent them so her knees were up.

His breathing was rapid as she heard the sounds of paper tearing and the snap of rubber.

A condom.

He was so careful, but she wanted to tell him not to bother, that it didn't matter to her.

How could anything that might befall her be worse than what already had? After losing him, she had often wished she had, instead of Harris, been the one to die.

But protection was important to Jonathan, and she wasn't sure she could speak right now, anyway.

His hands were holding her knees. "Are you ready?" His husky voice brought her back from the dark thoughts and drew a yes from her lips.

He dipped a finger in the wetness around her opening and dragged it up and down her folds. If he didn't stop, she would come before he went any further.

Had she said that aloud?

Because he did stop, and she focused on the feel of the coarse hair on his legs brushing the inside of her foot as he positioned himself between her legs.

And then his hardness pushed inside her, stretching her tender lips and muscles to thrust and bore further. Another release of wetness seeped from within at the pain, or rather, the pleasure, the relief of it as she took all of him.

Moans from a woman she didn't recognize escaped her throat over and over, involuntarily and noisily, as he reached her deepest limits.

Soon, her body began to quake and, once it started, so did his.

5

SHOPPING SPREE

I n the backseat of the dark sedan on his way back into the city, he pulled up a kink shop website on his phone and browsed the categories: blindfolds and masks; restraints; floggers and crops; paddles and slappers; leashes and collars; chastity devices; nipple clamps.

He knew she liked her hands tied. She liked being blindfolded. She liked pain with her pleasure. Just how much he wasn't yet sure, although his tired dick still managed to twitch with curiosity.

He suspected she might like humiliation, and he eyed a cluster of ball-gag images on the home page. But he loved hearing the sounds she made, and he wanted to be sure he would hear her if she told him to stop. He was unsure about her interest in electrical play but, considering his inexperience having his own gonads shocked, he made an executive decision to skip it, at least for now.

He needed to show her he could rise to the challenge after he faltered when she asked him to pull her hair.

She had gotten frustrated when he didn't understand it

at first, that she wanted pain. She asked him for that, to hurt, all night—both with and without words.

Whatever she needed, whatever kink she might be into, she had turned to him. He would be safe for her, and he would satisfy her. He would be worthy of her trust.

After she climaxed earlier, he had removed the blind-fold, untied her wrists, and rubbed them until she moved them away. He had brought her a warm washcloth and a towel and tried to clean her up, a risky move, he knew.

Sure enough, she waved him off.

"Will you come back?" she had asked, sleepy. "It's a long drive."

He had shaken his head in response. *It's nothing.* "Just say when."

Her question was his cue to go, and he bent to pick up his shirt.

He looked at her lying there, her chest rising and falling under the sheet she had covered herself with. She was still breathing heavily and undoubtedly sore. He had wanted to lean over and kiss her forehead before she fell asleep, but that would definitely be against her rules.

"Well, good night," he had whispered instead, shoving his hands in the front pockets of his jeans so he wouldn't succumb to the urge to touch her.

He had gone downstairs and let himself out, turning back to the front door to jimmy the handle while leaning his weight against the wood to make sure it was locked.

Now, in the darkness of the car, the website's checkout screen glowed with hope and possibility. Satisfied with his shopping spree, he clicked next-day delivery.

DUMBASS. He had forgotten to set the alarm last night, and now he was late.

It was almost ten o'clock when he got to the network—very professional—and lunchtime came early.

Rich leaned into the doorway of his office like he often did. "Sandwich shop's delivering. Working lunch." He pointed to the conference room. "We need to nail down the storyboards for Scandinavia."

For the next several hours, they laid out story arcs and itineraries around the people and places Jonathan planned to feature, with a few additions—advertisers, of course—after Clay, the showrunner, deemed to grace them with his presence.

On the rare occasions Jonathan watched a finished episode from start to finish, just how much work went into those forty-four minutes always surprised him.

When they broke around four o'clock, he slipped out to get some caffeine, skipping the first four coffee shops he passed to stay out in the fresh air a few minutes longer.

He darted into the fifth—surprisingly, there was no line—and left with a double espresso in one hand and a skinny soy latte, his assistant's favorite, in the other, propping the door with his shoulder for an incoming customer.

On the street, he turned uptown, glancing at the pedestrians coming his way before he realized one was staring wide-eyed right at him. Delphine.

"Hey," he started, "how are . . ." Her expression changed instantly from wondering to wounded, hurt clear in her eyes.

She turned away quickly, jaywalking into traffic.

A taxi squealed to a stop, and she pounded on the hood. "*Connard!*" he saw her yell, although he could barely hear it. *Asshole!*

That, he was sure, she intended more for him than the driver.

He didn't blame her. That he had thought about his cheating a lot since it happened was an understatement. And he still had not figured out the real answer: *Why?*

Because if you had asked him, right up to the point when he flirted with Anna and snuck into that fucking airport shower stall, he would have answered that—checkboxes all ticked—he had a fine marriage.

That he still hadn't identified the real reason for cheating made him question what kind of man he actually was—and whether he could trust himself to be loyal to someone new.

Mainly, it had been a theoretical question, until the last couple of nights of rock-your-world sex with Quinn. As much as he tried not to think beyond her next text, their chemistry ignited in him the prospect of more.

The phone vibrating with a call brought him back to reality as he crossed the intersection, and his dick perked at the thought it might be her. But she wasn't likely to get in touch this soon, and so far she preferred texting.

Still, hope and erection sprang eternal, and he took a seat on the next available bench, crossed his legs to hide the wood, and set down the coffee drinks beside him.

That's all the network needed—for him of all people to get stopped for public lewdness, or whatever it was called when you got a hard-on that might be apparent to random strangers on the street.

By the time he pulled out the phone, he had a waiting voice mail.

"Jonathan, hi. It's Leigh. Thanks again for coming to dinner at Quinn's the other night. She asked me for your number and said she might reach out to bounce ideas . . ."

He smiled at the unintended euphemism. If last night was Quinn's way of bouncing ideas, he would serve as her sounding board any time.

"... I'm just calling to ask you to encourage her however you can. She still seems fragile, but she needs to get another book written. Soon. She keeps saying her heart's not in it, but that needs to change. She needs to change that. Her publisher needs her to change that.

"She valued your input when you worked with us before. Could you maybe brainstorm with her or whatever she needs to push forward? Let me know if I can facilitate. And if you don't mind, no need to share with her I called."

He listened for a second longer once the message ended, expecting to hear an off-handed, "Toodles." Leigh was someone you could picture saying toodles.

He hadn't talked with Quinn about her writing; they hadn't talked, period. Should he tell her Leigh had called? Probably—he should be up front with her.

Besides, if she found out from Leigh instead of him, she would be pissed. Previous lesson learned; he would be honest.

But, was their ... their ... whatever this was, all twelve mind-blowing hours of it at last count, complicating things for her? She might need him as an escape, but he didn't want to distract her from her work. She was talented; the last thing he wanted was to stand in her way.

Wait, no. If he were being honest, the real last thing he wanted was for what they were doing to end.

SHE STOOD in the closet looking from the rack and shelving on the right side to the rack and shelving on the left side, trying to settle on a place to start.

But Harris's closet was a funhouse of cruel tricks and apparitions. His hanging suits were missing the body she could clearly see; his shoes lacked the feet and long, muscular legs she pictured striding confidently toward her; his casual shirts and neatly folded pile of jeans taken out of service. No longer required for his walks on the beach and into town for the farmers' market, Saturday café brunch, a visit to the hardware store.

She could still see in her mind his dirty handprints on the thighs from pulling stray weeds in the garden.

It should be impossible to be lost in such a small space. Because if she could sleep with another man, undress and stand naked before him and beg him to fuck her, shouldn't she be able to start sorting her dead husband's things?

Standing here, now, though, it felt as if her betrayal might be in the sorting more than the fucking. There was no way in, no way to begin this process of sectioning him from her life.

The sound of Leigh's ringtone interrupted and, for once, it inspired gratitude and motivation to answer, not dread. She raced out of the closet to her phone, tossed on the bed earlier.

"I know you won't like this," Leigh started in when Quinn answered, "but Nely wants to meet."

Her stomach lurched, although it was no surprise.

The publisher had been asking for an outline for months, and Quinn hadn't sent one; they asked for pages, and she didn't produce any. She requested an extension; they granted one. The new deadline was here, and the ball was in her court.

She was standing still while it bounced, then sputtered, past her.

Leigh continued. "They're trying to help . . . They want to see you get another book out. They want to discuss ideas together, you know, define a narrative arc so you have bones to work with . . . By the way, have you reached out to Jonathan?"

Writing on deadline had not daunted her before. Other writers described this experience too—the ideas seeming to come to her, not from her. She watched the movie play in her mind and took good notes, pausing to get a closer look at the colors and textures, to listen to the words, to figure out what was going on in the characters' heads and hearts.

That's where she had been the day Harris died, and for several days before, on a writing retreat at an artists' colony funded by a two-month Hollinger Fellowship to brainstorm, outline, and start her next book.

She hadn't wanted to leave him for so long, but the movie in her mind had pulled like a magnet, out of everyday life and into that mystical place where all she had to do was watch, listen, probe a little, and put it all to paper.

What she wouldn't give now to have had just one day, one hour, of that week back. One minute even, enough time to say a last goodbye.

"Can you hear me now? Hellooo?" Leigh's voice squawked through the phone.

"Yes, yes, sorry. The Bistro, for drinks and appetizers, four o'clock."

"Can I pick you up?" Leigh-code for *I'm worried you won't show.*

"That's okay. I'll be there," Quinn said, trying to sound reassuring. She *would* go to the meeting. She would keep an open mind about getting back to work, even though her heart had been emptied of words.

It wasn't only her heart; her whole being felt as if it had been turned upside down, emptied, shaken until there was nothing left, the contents of her old self ricocheting and scattering on the ground.

All the pieces of her stories too were strewn around her, but she didn't recognize them anymore. The glue, her grounding, her capacity to piece them together—gone.

Grief and guilt were the only things left inside, holding tight, unwilling to let go.

The house had been emptied, too. The furniture was there still, and all the things they had collected over their two decades. But where there used to be warmth and laughter and soulfulness, now there was only darkness, desolation, and cold, a trio as real and solid as stone.

Some days, she would stand on the balcony outside their room, her face turned toward the sun to try to remember warmth, but while her skin heated, the rest of her remained hollow and cold.

Maybe that's what this thing with Jonathan was about, this near-obsession with the feel of him inside her, with the bondage and the ache.

Otherwise, what kind of monster was she, still held underwater by grief but wet practically all the time, climbing the walls until he came to her again?

It was after noon when she ended the call with Leigh, but the last thing she felt like doing was eating lunch.

Instead, she stopped to plug in her phone to charge as she passed through the kitchen, slipped on the scuffed pair of garden clogs by the side door, and went outside.

She used to work here for hours pulling weeds, moving plants to sunnier or shadier spots so they would thrive.

Gardening used to be therapeutic, a hobby she would get lost in. Then the books took off, and her career followed, and she had hired a landscaping service.

Now she walked among the flowerbeds, the shade plants, the two raised beds of herbs. She should let the service go, although they kept it looking perfect.

Too perfect. She needed weeds to pull, dirt to dig her hands into, grit under her nails. She needed something productive, something meaningful, some fucking thing to do.

With the shears left on a railroad tie, she cut basil and parsley for a dinner she wouldn't cook and brought the fresh herbs into the kitchen, setting them down near the phone.

The phone.

You can't summon him every twenty-four hours.

He has a life, a career. Maybe a girlfriend, although that's not what the internet grapevine had said, and he wouldn't have left that small pack of condoms on her nightstand if he didn't want to come back, would he?

Just once more.

She picked up the phone, tapped out a text, and hit "send." It buzzed a moment later:

Leaving city in 30 min .

A FIERY SUNSET back-lit the approaching rain clouds, and she watched them from the covered deck. Soon a light drizzle began to fall, and she went inside, undressed, and put on her robe.

Each time she had texted him, she had struggled with what to wear. Jeans or her go-to yoga pants and a t-shirt would require the awkward step of undressing. Lingerie added to the guilt; it meant a deliberate effort at sexiness. The robe, it struck some kind of twisted balance.

Because sex, she should not be asking for sex.

Shoes presented a similar conundrum, again tonight. Barefoot, she felt too much like herself. She stepped into her black heels, the ones she had worn last time. Borderline slutty, but better.

In them, she could pretend to be someone else, someone better suited to booty-text an acquaintance to tie her up and fuck her hard, into a fleeting but necessary oblivion.

By the time headlights flared and she heard the crunching sound of tires on the driveway, the rain was pelting. She hurried downstairs and opened the front door to Jonathan, shaking droplets off his sleeves.

The water ran in rivulets down the worn caramel leather of his jacket. Drops slid down his face, dripped from the tip of his chiseled nose, trickled over his full lips. She held the door and stood aside to let him in—and so she could resist the urge to dry his body and taste the droplets on his eyebrow, his cheek, his mouth.

"Hey," he said in a hushed voice as he took off his shoes in the entryway, walked toward the living room, and lifted his messenger bag over his head.

She followed him and watched as he set the bag on the floor. He looked like he was about to ask her something, but he stayed quiet.

His hands went to her shoulders, turning her around so her back was to him, and he squeezed her upper arms. *Stay*.

He bent toward the bag, opened the flap, and when he stood again, blindfolded her. A shiver ran up and down her spine as he reached around and loosened the tie of her robe. The satin skimmed her calves as it fell to the floor, leaving her naked except for the instant rise of gooseflesh that covered her, head to toe.

There was more shuffling in the bag, and then he took her left wrist and, next, her right and brought them together behind her back.

Soft material brushed her skin as he bound her hands together at the wrists. The clink of metal—the post against his belt buckle?—sent moisture to the inside of her thighs, damp like the rain on his face a moment ago. Her breathing turned uneven, shaky in anticipation.

"You okay with this?" he asked.

"Yes." *Yes.* Need curled her hands into fists.

He ran his palm along her spine, around her neck, and wove his fingers through her hair, tugging—a signal, a tease.

With his hand at the base of her head, he guided her around to face him. Only ragged breathing metered their silence, his breath tinged with mint and with want. She knew desire well; she tasted it herself.

She sensed his gaze on her, taking her in, looking, planning.

And then his hands were on her hips, his long exhale tickling its way down her chest and belly. The robe brushed the tops of her feet as he moved it away. He was on his knees, his hands now on her thighs, pushing them apart. She stepped wider, craving whatever he was going to do.

"I have to taste you." His mouth on her skin dampened his voice.

He separated her lips and licked the length of her, ran his tongue along her folds and around her swollen bead. He bit lightly and she thrust her hips to feel more of his soft, warm mouth.

If her hands weren't tied, she would have to stop herself from running her fingers through his hair.

As if responding to her shifting, he pushed her legs wider apart and spread her further, the cool air adding even more sensation.

He explored with his lips and tongue, repositioning himself to gain better access. Sounds rose from her throat, her moans syncing with his hungry movements as he held her open, teased her, slid his tongue inside her.

When he stopped, she continued to move, aching to find him again, but he stilled her. She pictured him sitting back on his haunches, watching her once more.

But that wasn't all he was doing. His thumb pressed and circled her clit, wet from his mouth, wet from her own aching need.

After a few minutes he stopped, and she pictured him sitting back again. She could hear him catch his breath, but the absence of his touch created a void around her.

He came near again, and then his mouth was on her pussy, one hand on her hip, his fingers—first one, then two—sliding into her, careful but not gentle. Reaching, probing, deep.

The soreness from last night and the rhythm of his mouth and hand together brought her close to coming.

Her knees softened underneath her. He must have felt it, because he wrapped an arm around her waist to better support her.

His knuckles pressed her inflamed lips as he moved inside her, deep and deeper, rather than in and out. She focused on the ache and the heat, but her hands tensed against the restraints, instinctively wanting to move them in front of her body to brace against him.

She was so close, and he must have sensed it because he tightened his arm around her. But she didn't want to climax this fast.

Hadn't he just gotten here?

The rain on his face, the heat coming off him as he bound her hands, it wasn't long ago, or maybe she had gotten lost in time.

As if he had heard her, he answered her thought with an order, a deliberately spoken order she felt between her legs. "Unless you kick me out, you are by no means done for the night. Come. I want to watch you come."

He separated his fingers, spreading them so they filled more of her, pressed harder against her sensitive walls. His thumb hit her mound over and over.

When he finally spoke again, his voice was low and full of insistence. "Come for me."

Her breath caught in her chest as the waves of yet another powerful climax enveloped and erased her.

He kept massaging her slowly as her breathing slowed.

Once it did, he withdrew and, still supporting her, moved her toward the couch. His hand pressed on her back, guiding her to bend forward over the arm, like she had positioned herself last night, only this time her arms were bound behind her.

Now he was moving near her head, placing a pillow under her cheek.

He rifled in his bag and then he was behind her, bending, his breath tickling her calf. He tapped her ankle and helped her lift one foot and then the other to put on panties or, judging from how the fabric slipped between her cheeks, a thong.

Something cool pressed against her hypersensitive clit.

He adjusted the panty so it held the cold in place and pushed her legs further apart with his knee between them.

And then he moved away.

A flash of panic ran through her as he left her exposed and open, his footsteps receding.

The sound of water running told her he was in the powder room off the entry. A few seconds and it stopped. She expected to hear his footsteps returning, but he was quiet.

Until the faintest clicking noise emanated from the vicinity of her pussy, and then a whir, and the cold against her nub began to thrum.

Another click, and it oscillated faster. She involuntarily moved against it; the intense sensation so soon after coming was beyond arousing, and she cried out as it flooded her.

Over the whir, she heard his belt shoosh through his pant loops in one swift motion.

The sound was far enough away that he must still be by the bathroom. She pictured him leaning against the door-jamb, controlling her fervor with a remote, watching her reaction.

She was so wet, any second the toy would slip out of position, and she squeezed her thighs together to ensure it didn't.

His footsteps brushed against the carpet; he was coming closer. And then he slipped his hand between her legs, pushing them apart. Oh, she was going to . . .

The whirring stopped.

Maybe he wasn't going to let her come so quickly this time around. She heard the sound of a zipper, and—*please*—his clothes rustle to the floor.

Then he was rifling in the bag again, and her heartbeat thudded in her ears, but not loudly enough to drown out the electronic clicks, three in rapid succession. The whirring began again.

She turned her head, stifling her cries in the pillow he

had positioned for her. She was so dangerously close, she just needed a little more . . .

Another click, and she braced for more intensity.

But it stopped.

Damn it.

Her head sunk further into the cushion and she exhaled a deep breath, her heart racing from how he had yanked her back from the edge.

She heard the sound—a crack—before the sting registered, and she yelped, her voice sounding removed, distant.

Again she heard the sound and felt the sting. Leather against her ass.

His belt?

He kept going. The sensation heated, radiated through her body, warmth displacing the aching cold that had taken up residence inside her. She thrust her behind back toward him.

Again.

Soon she stopped counting the number of cracks, the stings, the pulses of fire and instead let herself float in the tempo of sound and sensation.

The heat radiated from his legs behind hers as he moved the thong to the side with his fingers, leaving just enough of the satiny material over her mound to hold the tiny vibrator in place.

His cock, covered in latex, nudged her lips apart, stretching her, bringing her down to earth.

He gripped her hips and slid deep inside her, then stood still.

Another click, and the toy was on again, vibrating against her while he withdrew and plunged hard. Her cheek chafed against the cushion with each thrust.

The sting and the heat radiated anew, exquisite. A frenzied cry escaped her mouth, a sound she didn't recognize, and her muscles gripped and held him deep inside her, pulsing as if she would never let go.

He came right after she did, but he didn't withdraw, and he didn't turn the toy off; it was vibrating wildly.

Was he trying to drive her mad?

It was way too much stimulation. *Stop*, she was about to tell him, but before the word could form, he placed his palm flat on her back, above her hands.

"Breathe," he coached, caressing her skin with his thumb. "Relax, and breathe."

She inhaled and focused on her breath. It helped push away the twinge in her chest from the intimacy of his whisper, from the gentleness of his touch.

He was still hard enough to thrust, deeper and deeper without leaving her pussy between strokes, and soon another orgasm rose within her and burst amid the rippling waves of the first.

When the contractions stopped, he pulled out of her slowly, took hold of her wrists, and began to unfasten the restraints. "Leave them," she said. "More."

"More?" He ran his fingers over the welts on her ass. "It was already too much."

"It wasn't."

"But don't you hurt enough?" His bewilderment was audible.

Enough? That would be impossible. "Please."

She heard shuffling and felt him behind her legs once more. Anticipation coursed through her, turning into solace as the sting of his belt or whatever he was using spread upward from her ass, along her spine, dulling the ache in her chest, her mind, her heart.

He hit her hard and repeatedly, until she was floating,

sinking, for some indefinable period of time, somewhere else.

A few droplets of the heavy water she felt submerged under seeped from her eyes. And then his hand was on her back, his body leaning over hers so she could feel his heat by her shoulder and his whisper in her ear. "Okay, we're taking a break."

He unfastened her wrists and removed the blindfold.

Her legs quivered as he helped her take a few steps away from the sofa to the rug, where she lay down on her side. A shiver prompted her to cross her arms over her chest, and he kneeled and reached for the throw blanket she kept draped over the couch. He covered her with it and put one of the softer cushions by her head.

When she didn't move, he carefully lifted her head at the temple with his palm and slid the pillow under her. She closed her eyes and felt him stretch out behind her, close but not touching.

As if by instinct, not choice—because she should not want this; she would not let herself want this—she scooted back until she felt him through the thin cotton of the blanket, until the soothing heat of his skin reached her and drew her body to his.

6

THE RIGHT ANSWER IS "NO, THANK YOU."

A familiar TSA agent waved him through security without having to take off his shoes. "Have a good trip, Mr. Jaines," he said, pushing the gray bin with Jonathan's laptop down the conveyor belt toward him.

At the gate, he and his team found a row of unoccupied seats, most with cracked blue cushions. The cushions weren't cracked in the frequent flier lounges, but since he had stopped being a dick, he no longer used his free upgrades when he traveled with his staff.

They set their bags down, and he offered to watch their stuff while they scattered for food, coffee, sleep masks, magazines.

As soon as they were gone, his mind beelined to the only place it now went when he had an unoccupied nanosecond: *Quinn*.

Since last night, he had not been able to stop picturing her, imagining the feel of her.

The little he knew of BDSM had never done much for him; he didn't get off on pain—inflicting or receiving—or on dominance. Others did, and that was cool as long as it was all consensual; whatever floats your boat, he didn't judge.

It was different with her.

How she made herself so vulnerable, how she let him know what she wanted those first couple of times and then put herself in his hands, how his sole focus became pleasing her, amping up the sensation, constantly checking that she was okay—it definitely did something for him now.

After he got to her house last night, as he blindfolded her and bound her hands, the gooseflesh rose on her arms and back, and she trembled in anticipation. He knew she would be wet, but when he put his mouth to her, wet was stating it mildly.

He made her come fast; that part was strategic. He was going to take his time the rest of the night—sweet, sweet time—and let the distinct sensations he had planned build into something greater than the sum of its parts.

Into something that would drive her wild. Into the something she had sought and chosen him to give.

If circumstances were different, he would have played a little more instead. He would have teased her by asking her if she wanted the vibrator turned on again, if she wanted his cock inside her, if she wanted it harder.

He would have listened for the desire in her voice as she answered him and savored it as he probed her mouth with his tongue.

He would have gotten her to come quickly and then teasingly punished her with the leather slapper for coming too soon.

He would have made her shudder again and, after she fell asleep, woken her gently and done it again.

He would have kissed the welts that rose on her ass,

pulled her on top of him, and fallen asleep with her body covering his.

He did none of those things.

It was not right to be playful or loving with her; she wanted neither.

But her intensity—he would not, as long as he lived, forget the sounds she made or how her body shuddered when she came, or how she squeezed and pulsed around him. He got hard whenever he thought about it, like there was a direct line between the image of her in his mind and the pre-cum seeping from his cock.

A guy with an airline logo on his navy sweater strode past him to the podium and made an announcement he didn't really hear.

Airport. Public space. Stop the instant replay.

He had not left her alone so fast last night. When they finished fucking, she still wanted him to smack her with the leather slapper he had bought—thank you, internet and overnight delivery. What they were doing had taken her somewhere else.

Instead of getting dressed and putting the toys back in his bag, he laid on the rug behind her and propped himself on his elbow so he could keep an eye on her.

Miracle of miracles, she had leaned back against him. Well, not exactly against, but close enough. He held still, fighting the urge to put his arm around her, to pull her closer, to do anything that might disturb their delicate equilibrium or break one of her rules.

While they lay there still and quiet, he remembered the call from earlier.

"Hey," he had said, giving her shoulder two delicate taps to ease the intrusion of talking. "Leigh left me a message today. She said you might be in touch about your book. She asked me to help you brainstorm . . . or whatever you need."

Quinn snickered, likely for the same reason he had. Tying her up, blindfolding her, smacking her ass until welts rose—probably not the help Leigh had in mind. "I called her to get your number."

"I would never say anything. About this, us. I'll tell her whatever you want me to tell her. But I do want to help if I can. With writing, I mean. We can talk through ideas or . . ."

She nodded and, another miracle, told him what was going on.

The publisher was pressuring her for a draft, at least some early pages, after she missed their extended deadline.

"I can't do it. It's just not there. And now they want to have some ridiculous meeting."

It was the most she'd spoken to him since the movie set, and he loved hearing her words, her voice.

"When's the meeting?"

"Next Thursday."

"Can you reschedule?"

He was coming home from his trip that day. "I could go with you, help bat around the ideas and maybe take some of the heat off you. They would know we've worked together on *Market Day*; it wouldn't necessarily seem weird that I was there."

The muscles around her shoulder stiffened, which told him it *would* seem weird—to her.

He touched her upper arm, brushing her skin lightly with the side of his thumb, a tiny reassuring gesture he made gingerly, without engaging his other four fingertips or, he hoped, violating any boundaries.

She had not pulled away. *Bingo.*

"That's okay. I can handle it. I have to." She looked over

her shoulder at him, one of the few times since the start of their arrangement, or whatever this was, that she had looked directly at him and not at something beyond him.

It was all he could do not to lean down, stroke her cheek, and kiss her.

She was upset about the meeting, and he wouldn't be in town to do anything for her. Maybe at least she and Leigh could spend a decent day in the city—have a glass of wine at a nice café, duck into a museum, see a Broadway show, people-watch from a park bench.

It might not be spanking or screwing, but he hoped she could enjoy a pleasant summer afternoon in Manhattan.

Or a night.

There was a definite change in how she was with him last night, and it emboldened him.

As the gate area grew busier around him now, he pulled the phone out of his breast pocket and double-checked his calendar.

He was flying home Thursday afternoon, scheduled to arrive at seven p.m. He pulled up their thread of text messages and started a new one to her.

At airport waiting for my flight out. I should be home by 8 next Thursday night. I'll text you when I land. Meet at my place since you'll be in the city? Have a good week.
Give 'em hell. -J.

He tapped "send" and, just as spontaneously, doubt arose.

Maybe it was too much. Maybe he should have waited a few days. Maybe he should play it cool, make her realize how much she wanted him.

But after last night, he knew she did; underneath the

distance and the rules, he saw her emptiness, sensed her need.

His text would let her know he would be there for her—in exactly the way she needed him to be—at the end of what promised to be a rough day.

No harm, no foul. At least he hadn't done anything dumb like suggest they have dinner first. A dinner where he could have an actual conversation with her over a good meal and a glass of wine, with dim lighting, flickering candles, soft, sexy music in the background . . .

Hello. Public space.

This was a friends-with-benefits thing only—she was clear about that.

Their wordless tango of control and surrender was some erotic fantasy come true. Still, it had been hard for him to hurt her purposely.

It wasn't so difficult for him to blindfold her, or to bind her wrists with the leather cuffs he'd carefully chosen for the cushy lining, or to strum her clit with maddening vibration as he stood back and watched her writhe.

But blindfolding, restraining, and whizzing a toy against her all fell into a different category, at least in his inexperienced mind, than consciously causing pain.

But that night of her dinner, she tapped him to play a role.

I sent your driver away.

He hoped to hell he could hold on to the part.

IN THE GARDEN, the beating afternoon sun warmed the top of her head, her face, her arms, and delicate early summer fragrance surrounded her—roses, peonies, lavender.

A furry bumblebee hovered and buzzed nearby while a seaplane droned in the distance, out over the ocean. With her forearm, she wiped the sweat from her cheeks and continued deadheading the peonies—stems thick and tough with age—that had bloomed early and now drooped over the edge of the patio.

The heirloom peony bushes had clinched their decision to buy the house almost two decades ago. She and Harris had toured it on a sunny Saturday around this time of year, when the blossoms' scent drifted through the open doors and windows.

"I want to live with you here," he had said.

The finances were a stretch for a promising but early-career lawyer, and she hadn't yet signed her first book deal.

Neither of them had any inkling of her forthcoming success, or the heartbreak it would bring. "We shouldn't," she had said. "The money . . ."

He allayed her caution with a kiss. "We can do it—we'll both love it here. We'll figure it out."

The bumblebee circled again as she cut the final stem with the pruning shears and stood to go to the roses. White spotlights filled her vision, the spinning reminding her she might have stood up too fast. She had been out here for hours now, without water or breakfast or lunch.

She got down again, sitting cross-legged in the shadow of a rosebush, and rested her head in her hands until the spinning slowed.

The scent of the flowers piqued her attention. She lifted her eyes and ran her finger along the browning petals of a spent blossom in front of her. She continued down the sepal to the stem with its sharp, smooth thorns, and tapped her fingertip against one.

A crimson droplet bloomed on her skin before she registered the prick of pain, a lot like how last night she had heard the crack of leather slapping her before she felt the sting.

And like how she had seen the quiet red welts on her ass in the bathroom mirror this morning before the falling water in the shower set them aflame.

She lived among the nuances of language, the many shades of meaning a singular word could possess, but until a few days ago, until Jonathan, she hadn't understood there existed such fine distinctions of sensation, of pain, each rare and extraordinary in its texture, each a world she wanted to explore from within.

She hadn't asked him to go last night, and he didn't leave until early this morning. Three a.m., or perhaps four; time was lost to her after what he had done to her body.

She didn't hear him get up and put on his clothes; she had only the fuzzy memory of her back suddenly cold under the blanket, until she slipped into sleep again, alone.

When she awoke, dust motes hung suspended in piercing rays of morning light.

And now her phone on the faded teak table vibrated with the sound of a text. She fantasized it was Leigh calling to tell her Nely had to cancel because of some emergency and reschedule for the first week of never.

Or Jonathan informing her his trip was postponed.

It was hard to say which of those scenarios she wanted more.

Only she did know.

She didn't smoke, always wore her seat belt, drank only socially and lightly, and rarely consumed more than a cup or two of coffee every morning. Her life was pathetically light on bad habits.

Except for Jonathan Jaines. He had hardly been gone from her house, from her body, for twelve hours, but he was becoming an addiction.

The phone was warm from the sun when she picked it up.

> At airport waiting for my flight out. I should be home by 8 next Thursday night. I'll text you when I land. Meet at my place since you'll be in the city? Have a good week. Give 'em hell. -J.

Last night she hadn't asked about his trip or his plans or how long he would be away; there had been something calming, untouchable, about their silence.

She sucked the droplet of blood from her finger and squeezed the pad until another emerged.

A week?

She put the phone in her pocket and kneeled by the bushes to gather the pulled weeds and cut stems into a pile. In the past she would have been careful to avoid the piercing thorns.

A week.

Into the big green garden waste bag they went, and she dragged the bag to the side of the house by the trash bins.

She went inside and upstairs to the bathroom. Okay, it might be good he was out of town, because there was no escaping the mess that stared back at her from the mirror.

Locks of stringy hair had fallen out of the rough ponytail she had gathered this morning; smudges of dirt marked her cheek and forehead; beads of sweat rested in the fine hair above her upper lip.

A week.

She washed her face and hands, the hands he had bound with what felt like leather cuffs last night. In the vanity drawer, she felt around for the vibrator she used to keep in there and turned it on.

It wheezed and fell silent.

She hadn't touched it since Harris died. Tending to her libido, once it stirred again after many months, had seemed wrong—disrespectful and trivial.

What was she supposed to think about while some silicone toy whirred inside her? Him? That was too painful, but it also had felt shameful to think about anything *except* him.

But more than a year had passed now, the fucking magic year after which she suddenly was supposed to be whole again, healed and ready to go on, a smile pasted from ear to ear.

Besides, she'd fucked another man. No sense worrying about disrespect and triviality any longer; shitty widow that she was, that line she had crossed.

She went downstairs to the utility room to find fresh batteries and snapped them into place.

With a press of the button, the toy buzzed to life. She turned it off and shimmied out of her jeans, leaving them damp with sweat on the floor in front of the washer.

Then she went up to the main level, to the couch where Jonathan had taken her last night. She lay back against the pillows and drew up her knees.

She still could not bear to think of Harris and, although she tried to imagine some nameless, silent, faceless stranger punishing her for her need, her mind kept returning to one face, one body, one man.

She slid the toy inside herself, fast and deep, and turned it on.

In her imagination, his breathing hitched when he discovered how wet she was, and he slapped her ass with leather when she asked him to punish her. She pumped the toy in and out, angling so she could reach her mound too, then plunged it in when she imagined him grunt and moan, thrust, and come.

With her free hand, she reached under her t-shirt and squeezed her nipple, digging her fingernail into the hardened flesh. Spreading her legs wider, she tilted her pelvis and imagined his quivering length slide even deeper inside her until it set her off too.

IN FRONT OF THE BISTRO, Leigh waved as Quinn emerged from the throng of early rush-hour pedestrians. She waved back, hoping the gesture would help her summon from within a degree of enthusiasm she did not possess.

They hugged and Leigh pulled back, still holding both her hands, a quick strategic huddle. "Just be open to their ideas," she said. "Assure them you're ramping up to your usual stride, and you're excited—" She let go of one hand to shake a rah-rah fist low in the air—"to get this next book written."

Inside the restaurant, blinding-white small plates held finicky starters. In the past, she would have appreciated the creativity, the effort. Now? So what?

For the next couple of hours, Quinn listened to Nely, two of her editors, and Leigh, nodding—convincingly, she hoped—at their thoughts about the next book.

The ideas were all over the place. Irony, melancholy, wit, a woman on a journey, a man on a journey—were they serious?

Quinn uncrossed and re-crossed her legs and stifled an exhausted yawn, quickly covering her mouth with her napkin.

In all the years she'd worked with this imprint, they wanted original, *prided* themselves on publishing original. That's why they had signed her.

But what were they tossing around over shot glasses of cold soup and grilled exotic fruits? One cliché after another, heightened only by how excited they seemed with their concepts.

As with the food, she couldn't get herself to feel a single damn thing.

It went on in the same vein until Nely said she needed to get to another engagement.

The check was brought to the table and paid and a conference call scheduled in two weeks' time. Smiles, handshakes, stilted hugs. *Looking forward to seeing your work.*

Outside the restaurant on the busy street, Leigh put her hand on Quinn's back. "How about we find somewhere to sit?" She pointed across the asphalt toward the park, as pairs of women power-walked after work and a rollerblader wove among them in the rosy-gold dusk.

They found a bench and sat, and Leigh turned to her. "So. What do you think about all the promising ideas?"

By Leigh's and the others' measures, it had gone well. Excellent discussion, a proposed direction, a nice, clean narrative structure.

She picked at a chip of paint flaking from the bench, trying to form a response, but Leigh wasn't done. "Do you think you have something to work with now?"

A sharp paint chip pierced the skin between her fingertip and nail. What was the point of continuing this way?

"Honestly? No, if you want to know the truth."

Leigh's mouth moved as if forming words, but none came out. She looked as though she were trying on sentences in a cramped dressing room, but nothing fit quite right.

Finally, she found two sentences that did, and her beaded earrings bobbed as she shot them at Quinn: "Are you ready to throw away your career? Because, if you do not make more of an effort to get back at it, that's what you'll be doing."

"I realize that."

Leigh's shoulders dropped. "Why? I mean, how . . . How can you let it all go, just like that?"

Just like that?

Anger squeezed Quinn's windpipe, tightened her voice. "Jesus, Leigh, I didn't take a year off on some whim and disappear to Fiji for a little break."

"I know." Leigh touched Quinn's forearm and rubbed, trying to soothe but looking more like she wanted to remove a stubborn spot. "It was a horrible, horrible tragedy. I hate to be the one to say this, but . . ."

Life goes on.

How many times had she heard some diplomatically paraphrased riff on that in the past year from many people who claimed to care about her?

"You're at a crossroads," Leigh said. "You have a choice to make. You get back to work and you write a book—soon— or you break your contract and take a giant step backward in your career and hope, *hope*, a publisher, and readers, will give you another chance *when you're ready*."

Leigh said *when you're ready* like Quinn actually had chosen this, chosen to gut her life.

"I know what's at stake, but it doesn't come out of thin air." She pressed her hand against her chest. "It's empty. *I'm* empty. I'm sorry to let you down."

She got up to leave, but Leigh grabbed her arm before she could dart into the flow of strangers and disappear.

"Don't run off—I'm trying to help. I know you can't think about the future right now, but as your agent, and as your friend, that's where I have to focus *for* you."

Leigh lightened her hold.

"You're right. I can't think about the future right now." This time she was faster, and Leigh's hand missed her arm as she bolted.

———

SHE WALKED until it was dark and the tears cleared. That was an underappreciated charm of Manhattan, that you could cry while you walked down the street and not feel terribly self-conscious because no one seemed to notice.

Or, if they did, they knew to leave you alone.

In a coffee shop, she wiped crumbs from a small round table with the edge of the rumpled alternative weekly someone had left behind. She pulled out a chair, sat, and checked her phone.

Nothing from Jonathan. It was almost nine, an hour later than he expected to be back.

He's delayed. Give him some time.

She wished she could text him and have him appear, blindfold her, bind her, take control, use his body to free her.

She opened the paper and read the headlines, mindlessly turning from page to page.

The man at the next table cleared his throat, and she glanced in his direction. He was glaring at her foot, and she stilled the jittery tapping, the heel of her pump against the chair leg like a nervous baby bird's flapping wings.

She didn't want to go home. She needed Jonathan tonight, needed to have him inside her, his marks on her. Needed to take what he would give her. It had already been a week. A long week. She would go insane if she had to wait another day.

She turned the paper over to leaf through it from the beginning.

Check the phone again. Maybe you didn't hear it.

Still nothing. She set the phone back on the table alongside the open paper. As she aimlessly browsed the ads, one caught her eye.

Octavia's

Safe. Discreet. Welcoming.

She had heard of Octavia, the dominatrix who ran an upscale BDSM club; one of the city's highbrow culture magazines ran a profile of her a few years back.

Which magazine escaped her, but she did recall being surprised by the article, by how down to earth Octavia and the club—the dungeon—had sounded, how . . . approachable.

If you were curious about the dungeon scene and wanted to check one out.

Not that she had any basis for comparison. Her sex life with Harris had been satisfying but definitely vanilla, except for a little playful spanking now and then.

She could still remember the fleeting thought she had when she had read that profile: If she and Harris were ever going to experiment, Octavia's seemed like a place they would be comfortable getting started.

The phone sat quiet as a mouse on the table in front of her, but she turned it over and checked again, anyway.

Cold air blew on her from the air vents, interrupted by a balmy breeze whenever someone opened the door. She should go outside, get some air, move her body after sitting all day.

Before setting the phone down again, she tapped out the letters in the web browser search bar.

It turned out Octavia's wasn't far, practically around the corner.

A note in bold text on the website explained that first-time visitors should complete the online application, then wait for a text-message link to download an app. The app unlocked the door once you were outside the club.

Quinn appreciated the security, but she didn't need the application or the app—she was not going inside Octavia's; she was just taking a walk in that direction to pass the time while she waited for Jonathan to land.

She closed the paper, put the all-too-quiet phone in her purse, hoisted the straps onto her shoulder and left the coffee shop. Despite the darkness, it was still hot out, and a trickle of sweat slid between her breasts.

As she got closer to Octavia's, the butterflies in her stomach switched from flitting to panicked acrobatics.

Just passing by.

A small silver-gilt rococo Octavia's sign hung on a lamp-post outside a stately brownstone. Swirls on the staircase's wrought iron balusters, two well-tended garden patches on either side of the steps, ivy raining down from the window boxes—it would be easy to mistake for a private residence if you weren't looking for it.

Not that she was looking *that* hard for it.

Burgundy drapes covered the front windows, concealing the view inside.

Oh, for goodness' sake, what was she doing here?

With her black A-line skirt and black and white polka dot blouse, she was more appropriately dressed for a job interview at a library, not a visit to a dungeon.

But she was not visiting a dungeon. She had just walked by because she happened to remember that article.

Although, if she *were* to poke her head in for a second, for curiosity's sake, at least she was wearing black, and her heels were high. In the profile, the writer had made a big deal about how Octavia's members came from all walks of life and experience levels, how it wasn't all leather and latex, that patrons often showed up in their street clothes. Why had that detail stayed with her?

She reached into her bag and checked the phone again.

Where was Jonathan? She pictured how he tied her hands and surprised her with sensations that wiped her emotions clean. If only that state of obliteration had lasted longer, if only she could have bottled it for when he was away.

She saw two choices. She could go back to the coffee shop, order another latte, tap her foot, and sit there in damp panties, hoping he would text soon, or she could go home to that empty house, alone with too many memories.

Actually, there was a third choice. She could enter her information in the fields on Octavia's secure website, download the app, and unlock the door. Just out of curiosity, just to pass some time.

Only once.

She took a deep breath, followed the instructions online, and tapped the app's "I'm here" button when it appeared.

The lock on the heavy wooden door under the stoop clicked and, squaring her shoulders, she pulled it open.

THE WOMAN at the reception desk smiled warmly, the kind of greeting you wished for at the doctor's office but rarely got. "Hi there, I'm Vanessa." She extended her hand across the marble countertop. "You're new."

"I am," Quinn said nervously.

"Well, welcome." Vanessa's eyes sparkled in the dim light, and her smile put Quinn at ease.

Vanessa asked to see Quinn's ID while the printer behind her spat out a sheaf of pages. She picked up the stack and slid it across the counter.

Club rules.

The first three paragraphs, all bold type and italics, emphasized confidentiality. What happened at the club stayed at the club.

No problem agreeing to that; it wasn't like she would bump into anyone she knew here.

The other rules were similarly straightforward—only one person or party at a time in the club's anteroom and dressing room in order to protect members' privacy. Solo members welcome (everyone welcome), nudity and sex allowed *only* on level three, don't interrupt a scene, no touching whatsoever without consent, no food in the play areas but the kitchen is stocked with sparkling water and snacks. No alcohol. No drugs. No ridiculing others' preferences or scenes.

One visit allowed on a provisional basis while the club conducted a background check. Assuming it turned up nothing concerning, a board member would be in touch to extend an offer of membership.

"Oh, membership won't be necessary." Quinn glanced up at Vanessa. "I'm just here to . . . just for . . . tonight."

Vanessa smiled like she might hear people say that a lot. "Of course. You can always decline the offer and re-activate your application if you change your mind."

Quinn finished reading and signing the rules and handed the pages back. "I'll text Alex," Vanessa said. "He's one of our DMs—sorry, dungeon monitors—tonight, and he'll show you around. Everyone's really friendly and cool here, but if you have any questions, see Alex or me. Octavia's on the floor tonight too. I'm sure she'll come find you to introduce herself."

Alex emerged from behind a velvet burgundy curtain that separated the reception area. He was a few inches taller than Quinn and at least a decade younger. His clean-shaven face, black t-shirt and black jeans shouted *boy band* more than *dungeon monitor*. Although she had never known any dungeon monitors—at least none she had been aware of.

He led her back to the main floor, a large open central area with a high ceiling and a glittery chandelier at the center. Semi-private nooks lined the perimeter, with delicate sconces casting a warm glow from the pillars between each alcove.

Off the main floor, Alex showed her the restrooms and additional changing areas, the equipment closets, and the kitchen, waving or nodding to just about everyone who wasn't immersed in something else.

He took her from station to station, hanging back behind the people gathered to watch each scene.

At the first, a woman wearing a black corset that

appeared to be made of rubber was shackled to an A-frame stand, while a man teased her thighs with a long feather.

In the second bay, a man padlocked a cage with another man on all fours inside it. In the nook across the room sat an unoccupied medical table with stirrups.

A woman in stiletto heels and a hospital gown, open in the back to reveal a thin strap of thong, and a man carrying a black doctor's bag headed toward it.

To Quinn's left, Alex pointed out a large, dark wood frame with chains arranged like a spider web. She imagined the cold metal against her wrists and ankles—and what Jonathan might do if he were the one who had put her there. A shiver shot through her body.

"Mahogany," Alex told her with more than a hint of pride. "Hand made. We found this artisan in Germany who crafts our furniture. Each piece is one of a kind."

"It's beautiful." The dark wood was gorgeous. "He must be talented." Although when Alex next showed her the padded wall, she couldn't help but have one criticism: *Why did it have so much cushioning?*

Alex paused by the staircase, restricted with a burgundy-braided rope between two stanchions, reminding her of the entrance to a theater.

"So. Upstairs." He pointed. "Nudity and sex are okay on level three. There's an open common area with some couches and day beds, and then around the outside, we have the private rooms. You can reserve one at the front desk or in advance through the website. Want a quick tour?"

"No, thank you," she said, shaking her head. "I'm fine down here."

She was just checking the club out; she was not going to actually do anything or take off her clothes or have sex with a stranger.

Jonathan had already spiked her guilt like a deliriously bad fever. What she wanted was to escape, and despite all the padding, she could do that down here.

If she were going to do anything. Which she wasn't.

"Well, I'll let you do your thing." Alex met her eyes. "Or can I help you find a play partner? People are super-approachable, but I'm happy to make introductions if you're more comfortable that way."

Beyond walking in the club's front door, she had not planned on having to make decisions or answer questions.

That was one of the main reasons she had texted Jonathan after that first night—and after each of the rest—even though she had sworn it was the last. He had an uncanny way of knowing what she needed; she didn't have to ask, and neither did he.

"I'm good. Thanks for the tour."

Alone now, she slowly circled the large room again, pausing at the back of the groups watching the scenes unfolding in the alcoves.

Closer to the middle of the room, people mingled and talked as if it were any other gathering. And just like she felt less awkward at those gatherings with a glass of wine in her hand, she should go to the kitchen to get a glass of water.

A cracking sound redirected her attention and she turned toward it. A woman in a black bodysuit was bent over a red padded sawhorse, her wrists in cuffs, each fastened to a metal ring on the legs.

A man stood behind her, bringing a flogger down on her ass again and again. The woman's mouth moved each time, but the ethereal electronica coming through the ceiling speakers drowned out the sound.

It didn't matter. From the look on her face, Quinn could practically hear her moans of pain and pleasure.

She joined the growing group of onlookers. A second man she hadn't noticed was standing beside the woman, holding a lit candle above her back. Drops of white wax slid down her torso and around her ribs, slowing and hardening.

The two men worked in tandem, one flogging, one dripping molten heat. A tingle electrified Quinn, her own torso getting warmer just from watching.

"It's a work of art," a woman whispered, interrupting Quinn's awe at the exoskeleton of cooled wax.

"It's incredible," she agreed, turning toward the voice. Although a few years had passed, she recognized Octavia immediately from the photos that had run with that profile —the long, black corkscrew curls and astute dark brown eyes that didn't miss a detail, but also didn't make you feel you were being watched.

"Do you want to try it?" She gestured toward the scene. "I'm Octavia, by the way. Vanessa said we had a guest. Very nice to meet you. Do you go by Quinn, or do you prefer a scene name, a pseudonym?"

"Quinn's fine—and it's nice to meet you, too." The hand Octavia extended to shake hers was strong and kind, warm and confident.

"Are you here with anyone?"

"No, I'm alone." She forced a smile.

"I can show you what it's like if you're curious."

The right answer is, "No, thank you."

She was only here because Jonathan wasn't home yet.

She needed him again. If she were completely honest, she *wanted* him again.

The last night they were together, before he went away, she had felt a pull, an overpowering force, and she had let herself lean into him. She hadn't wanted him to leave, although she didn't tell him that.

Unlike their previous encounters, that night was about more than the escape he had given her; if she were completely honest, it was also about *him*.

And she could not—would not—let herself want it. Because she was still grieving. Because she still loved Harris. Because she never wanted to experience another loss of this magnitude again, ever.

"Yes, please."

"Then follow me," Octavia said, cocking her head toward an alcove with a neatly made massage table and, thankfully, no crowd around it. "I'll get a candle."

7

YES, TONIGHT

The city's buildings twinkled in the darkness as ribbons of white headlights and red taillights snaked along the gnarled highways. Bridges and skyscrapers jutted into the sky, their outlines visible by the dabs of light, a giant connect-the-dots in high-wattage bulbs.

The view from the air always gave him a rush. It also reminded him he was one lucky son of a bitch to have landed this gig—and to have kept it by the skin of his teeth.

As the flight attendant passed by collecting trash, he handed off the remains of a perfectly good gin and tonic before the turbulence sloshed it into his lap. He turned his wrist to check the watch face yet again.

Now he was over an hour fucking late. No way Quinn would wait.

One ear popped while he mentally kicked himself for not texting her before they took off.

He had sprinted through three terminals and still was the last to board and squeeze into his seat as the plane began to taxi to the runway.

Then there was this past freaking *hour* of circling over

Manhattan. He should have given her his address and told her to go to the apartment earlier; Barnes would let her in. She could be sitting on his couch or laying in his bed when he came home, waiting, ready for him, wet with anticipation.

Now? He had to get his head around the disappointment—the evening he had been looking forward to all week was not going to happen.

But a man could dream. He shifted his jacket and the book he was reading to better cover his lap. In this respect, it was good his crew had been booked on other flights.

The captain's voice came over the loudspeaker. Finally, the air traffic had thinned, and they were cleared to land.

The second those tires skidded to a halt on the tarmac, he turned his phone on and texted her.

> Sorry! Just landed. You still in the city?

He put the book and jacket in his backpack and ducked out of his row and toward the nearest exit. The phone buzzed in his shirt pocket while he was walking down the jet bridge to the terminal, and he quickly fished it out.

> Website says flight is in. Usual meeting place.

Reliable Gil—he was a great guy. But unfortunately, not Quinn.

The ribbons of red and white lights looked a lot less pretty and twinkly from down here when you were stuck in the middle of them.

Almost an hour of stop-and-go traffic later and no incoming texts, he dragged his small, rolling carry-on into the empty apartment. At least there was some light and—he quickly pressed the remote—sound from the TV. He sat on the couch for a few minutes and set his phone on the coffee table.

He should take a shower, wash the stink of stale plane air off himself in case she was, by some miracle, still in the city. Put clean sheets on the bed. Chill a bottle of wine. Maybe she would accept a glass, although he doubted it.

He checked the phone again. The screen was dark. He leaned his head back against the cool leather.

A distant siren roused him from the sleep he had not intended. He picked up the phone from the coffee table. It was four in the morning. Maybe she hadn't gotten his text. Or maybe she was pissed he had been late.

He composed a new one.

> Very sorry about ruined plans. Make it up to you
> tomorrow (tonight)? Sleep well. -J.

On second thought, he added "xo" before his name. More intimate, but still fairly noncommittal.

On third thought, he deleted it. "Sleep well" was intimate enough for her. He pictured her soft skin and dark eyelashes beneath her closed lids and his dick half-heartedly stirred as he stretched out on the couch and fell back asleep.

She didn't text until sometime after lunch. He had been so obsessively checking his phone at the office all morning that Rich took it from him as they went into an eleven o'clock meeting.

"Chill, dude," he'd whispered, lifting it from Jonathan's hands. "Whoever she is, she'll have to wait."

> Yes, tonight.

WIDE BEAMS of morning sun streamed in the bathroom window and ricocheted off the white tiles as Quinn twisted to see her back in the mirror. No evidence of the wax. Of course not; Octavia was a pro.

At the club last night, she had pulled a heavy velvet curtain that Quinn hadn't noticed across the nook with the massage table, giving her privacy. "If you're comfortable, you can take off your shirt and unhook your bra and lie on your stomach."

Octavia talked through everything she was doing in her soft, assured voice—spreading the fire-retardant blanket, putting an extinguisher next to the table just in case, making sure their hair was out of the way of the candle's dancing flame.

As Octavia massaged a thin layer of warm oil into Quinn's back so the wax would peel off easily, tears welled in her chest. Octavia's expert hands had felt so good, reminding her how deeply she had missed being touched.

Basic, human touch.

Not Jonathan's searing sexual touch that came at such a high price—a mountain of guilt and fear.

Although, the fear she could let go because a relationship with him was simply a non-starter. She would never again open herself to love like she had with Harris; she would never again let herself be cleaved in two.

The heat on her back and Octavia's occasional soothing words dulled the feelings she didn't want to have. She could focus intensely on each drop of wax, the sound it made as it landed on her skin, how it rolled and slowed and hardened.

Sometimes a droplet would catch a fine hair and she would concentrate on the delicate tug. All of it—the sound of Octavia's voice, her words, the safety measures, the sensations—reduced to essentials.

When she was done, Octavia asked if she wanted to see it. At her yes, Octavia used the camera on her phone to show her the droplets and their trails, hardened on her body like armor.

Octavia had stayed with her in their alcove, asking how she felt and if she needed anything, and then she sat on a stool in the corner and busied herself on her phone while Quinn rested and drifted, not really asleep, not really awake.

After some time, of which Quinn lost track, Octavia touched her shoulder and asked in a whisper if it was okay to peel the wax off her back.

She could still feel it there in her imagination, the protective layer, the second harder skin.

Even now, the next afternoon, even at her own house, even with the whining, intermittent buzz of the landscaping company's weed cutters below her bedroom window.

Amid the noise, the sound of tires on the stone driveway rose. *Jonathan?* She hurried along the hall and down the stairs to the front door.

Through the sidelight windows, she saw the once-familiar blue van with the white letters parking in front of the house. *King Dry Cleaning. Give Your Clothes the Royale Treatment.*

She used to joke with Harris about the typo, about how the van needed a copy editor to remove the E on royale.

The truck hadn't been to the house in more than a year, and she didn't recognize the driver who was coming toward her, carrying a stack of shirt boxes.

"Mrs. Layborn?" He glanced at the yellow slip taped to the top box. "My boss found some items of yours in our

Unclaimed room. Actually, looks like they're for your husband. Says here we tried to contact him several times."

She looked at the slip with its running list of dates, "Left msg," scrawled beside each.

The driver shrugged. "I had a delivery nearby, so I thought I'd drop them off." He was looking at her, expecting her to do something, but her hands were frozen in place.

"I . . . I'll leave them here for you if that's okay," he said, motioning inside the doorway. "Or, wait, is there another address I should bring them to instead?"

She could read his thoughts. *Maybe the guy doesn't live here anymore.*

"No, here's fine; I'll take them." She couldn't bear to send anyone away holding something of Harris's in his hands.

She stepped aside to let him in, and he set the stack just inside the door. As he walked out, she closed it behind him before leaning against it and sinking to the floor, the hard wood cool against her back as she wept.

8

BEGINNER'S LUCK

It might have been the longest afternoon of his career, although somehow he had managed to download his photos and videos from the trip and, with Rich's input, select the ones they would use for upcoming blog and social media posts and trailers. After the meeting he tried to write some of the content and the voice-over script for the show, but that was way too big an ask for his Quinn-addled brain.

By six-thirty, he was heading down the block for a takeout sandwich, which he wolfed down on the walk back to the office. A quick tooth-brushing, and he packed up, rode the elevator to the lobby, and was sitting in the thick of rush-hour gridlock with Gil by seven.

It had been over a week since he'd seen her; he should have taken the damn train.

When he finally got there, she opened the door and let him in. "Hi," he whispered. She wore that silky black robe that stopped just above her knee. "I'm sorry again about last night."

"It's fine." She waved off his apology, eager to change

the subject. He was starting to know her micro-expressions, her tells, and he wanted to learn more. He wanted to learn *her*.

"Your trip okay?" Her voice and her eyes seemed sadder than he remembered.

"Yeah, it was good. Hectic." He slipped off his shoes as he answered and noticed a stack of shirt boxes near the door, as if they'd been tossed there and forgotten. That didn't seem like her.

Once they reached the living room, he set down his messenger bag and removed the blindfold, which he'd tucked in an outside pocket for quick access. "But it was too long." He stepped behind her to tie the satin.

He wanted to say he had missed her, that he could not wait to see her. He wanted to kiss the soft skin along the length of her neck.

But he didn't.

Instead, he reached for her arms and brought them behind her back, holding her wrists together with one hand. With the other, he picked up his bag and slung it over his shoulder, then guided her slowly up the staircase.

He led her into the bedroom, and once she stood beside the bed, he slipped the robe off her shoulders and helped her down, positioning her on the mattress on her back.

This time, he buckled the restraints he'd brought around her ankles and watched her shiver at the sound the straps made as he stretched and tied them to the bedpost.

"Scarves in your nightstand?" he asked on a whisper. That's where she took them from last time, but he didn't want to go through her things without asking.

She nodded yes.

He found them easily and, sitting beside her, tied her

wrist to the bedpost before walking around the bed and doing the same on the other side.

His cock strained against his jeans as he stood and looked at her spread-eagled before him. He undressed and went downstairs without saying a word.

He was quiet in the kitchen and on his way back up the steps so she wouldn't know what he was doing. Hell, he didn't know what he was doing.

But between the internet, his imagination, and watching her reactions since that first night, he had several ideas to pilot.

In the bedroom again, he straddled her thighs and, quietly, took an ice cube out of the zip-top bag he placed beside him on the bed. A cube in each hand, he held them over her breasts until the ice started to melt.

The first drop hit precisely on her nipple—beginner's luck—and she gasped and flinched.

Another drop plinked against her sensitized skin, and then another. He bent and took a cold, erect, beautiful nipple in his mouth, first sucking, then teasing with his teeth. He alternated breasts, alternated the heat of his mouth with the chill of the ice, aiming the cold drops over her smooth belly in between. Her skin quivered and rose in tiny bumps in response.

He stopped to let her feel the sensations, like the dramatic pause an acting coach had taught him, but soon he let the drops fall on other parts of her body—the side of her neck, the inside of her wrist, the top of her foot, her thigh, the area right above her pubic bone.

She inhaled a deep breath when he bent over her to suck the drops off her skin, and he teased her even more by running his index finger, only once, lightly along her folds.

She gasped and canted her hips, wanting. From her clit to her entrance, she was as wet as he was hard.

When the ice cubes melted away, he untied her wrists, undid the ankle restraints, and guided her onto her stomach. Sitting back on his heels between her calves, he spread her legs wider, cupping her ass and feeling her skin against his palms and thumbs, learning her body.

He dragged his fingertips down the back of one thigh and, when she let out another faint moan, did the same on her other leg. He could spend all night right here, focused on the rise of her calves, the sensitive skin behind her knees, the backs of her thighs, exploring every inch of her legs, not to mention where they led.

Quietly, he took the slapper from his bag, pretty damn pleased with himself for remembering to leave it open on the bed so he wouldn't have to leave her, even for a few seconds, to retrieve the toys. With his other hand, he rubbed and squeezed her ass cheek, giving her some sensation for context before swinging the leather against her skin. She yelped, clearly not expecting it.

When he could see her muscles relax, he swung it again, and she arched her ass toward him to meet his strike.

It grew rhythmic, their cycle of sound and stillness, tension and release, until after an especially hard slap she arched toward him once more, and he couldn't stand it any longer.

He took a condom from the other front pocket of his bag, hustled it on fast, and positioned himself behind her.

"Are you ready?"

"Yes."

That was all he needed. Lifting her hips and holding fast, his eyes stayed glued to her slick opening as he slid inside her and reveled in her moan.

999, 998 . . . If he didn't go slow, he would be done in a flash, an embarrassingly fast flash.

"Harder," she pleaded, her voice muffled by the sheets she was gripping.

He sped up, thrusting harder and deeper. His cock swelled even more at the sound of her sighs.

"Hit me."

He slowed his pace for a second to reach for the slapper and hit her as he pulled out, then thrust back into her and swatted her again as he pulled out. Not very smooth, but harder each time as he found the tempo. Thrust, slap, thrust, slap, thrust, slap.

"My face. Slap my face." She ripped off the blindfold and swept her hair off her damp face before twisting around to give him a clear shot at her cheek.

He dropped the slapper on the bed and, still inside her, laid his palm on her back. "Not your face." *What the hell?* "I can't."

"Slap my face!"

Her voice was full with despair and frustration, just like when she had asked him to pull her hair. His cock twitched inside her, it too remembering how she had cried out and came soon after he yanked it.

Instead of slapping her face—no fucking way—he reached for the back of her head, knotted his fingers in her hair, and yanked hard and fast.

A popping sound came from near her neck, and something landed on the sheet next to her. His eyes flew open; her hand shot to the base of her neck.

Fuck. Her heart necklace.

He winced at the awful whimpering sound she made.

"It's okay, I'll have it fixed tomorrow," he offered quickly, trying to hold on to her hips and pull out of her gently as she struggled against him. "Here, let me take it and get it fix—"

She bolted upright to sit cross-legged on the bed, her back to him. "You need to go," she said, her voice cracking between sobs.

"Hey, hey, calm down." He sat on the bed and rubbed her back. "It was an accident. It can be fixed. I'll bring it back to you tomorrow."

He would take the morning off from work, find a jeweler who could fix it on the spot, and deliver it back to her straightaway. The city was big—he would find someone to take care of it.

She knocked his arm away. "It *can't* be fixed. You can't fix it. You could have done what I asked, not . . . this." She thrust her hand toward him, the slack chain draped over her palm, two of its delicate links stretched open and twisted.

"Go," she repeated. Breaking the necklace was symbolic, a metaphor—he got that. But she was getting more upset, and his continued presence seemed only to make it worse.

"Okay, I am. I'm going," he said, climbing off the bed, fumbling to pick up his clothes. "I'm sorry."

But wait, what exactly was he apologizing for?

Anger rose in his throat. "I'm sorry I'm not some lowlife who gets off on hitting women; I'm sorry I won't smack you around."

He waited for her to say something more as slowly he walked out of the room and down the hall, but she was quiet except for the weeping.

His chest hurt hearing her. He wanted to go back and comfort her, hold her and rub her back until she stopped, but . . . This was Quinn, and that would not happen.

He threw on the rest of his clothes by the top of the stairs and went down, let himself out the heavy front door.

She was still quiet when he texted her later that night and the next morning and the next evening and he stopped trying when he lost track of how many days after that.

WHEN HE GOT Leigh's voice mail inviting him to dinner at her apartment in two weeks, he called back immediately to accept. He wasn't in any mood for a party, but maybe by some miracle Leigh might convince Quinn to come.

He arrived in time for cocktails in her high-ceilinged living room. Stark white walls, enormous paintings, a dark wood floor—decor as unique in the city as a private school uniform.

Quinn was not there. No surprise. Although any time another guest walked in, he turned to look, pathetically hopeful.

After a while they moved into the dining room, and he found his place card between two writers whose names he vaguely recognized and across from Leigh. She was standing with her hands on the back of her chair, watching everyone as they took their seats before she retreated to the kitchen to bring out the food.

Once she sat, he waited what he hoped was an unre-markably short time before catching her eye amid all the chatter to ask how Quinn was; he didn't want to sound as eager as he felt.

"She's not answering my calls," Leigh said, her frustration obvious from her face, her voice, her sigh as she spooned something green with quinoa onto a plate. "So I'm giving her space. I just wish she could . . . hoist herself above this."

He waited to hear it: *It's been over a year*. To her credit, if she was thinking it, at least she didn't say it.

The two writers made sympathetic sounds and frowny it's-just-so-sad faces. One shifted in her seat, cleared her throat, and shot a furtive glance that started in his direction and quickly continued around the table, as if she were checking to make sure others weren't listening. "I heard she's been, um . . . going to visit Octavia."

The woman looked at the author next to her and then at Leigh. Her tone was funny, her look conspiratorial; he pictured her nudging their elbows, although she didn't actually.

"What's she doing at"—Leigh was interrupted by an unseen motion generated somewhere under the table. Water shimmied in unison in the glasses at their end of the table, and Leigh's forehead contracted. "I mean"—cough—"I didn't know Quinn *knew* Octavia."

Octavia.

The name was familiar, and he thought about the mutual acquaintances in their slightly overlapping social circles, but he couldn't come up with a last name. Nor could he conjure a face.

"Well, apparently they do"—ahem—"know each other. Someone mentioned it at my last writers' group meeting. A friend of a friend said she'd seen the *Market Day* author at . . . I mean visiting . . . Octavia."

"Hmm," Leigh uttered. "Maybe they confused her with someone else."

The conversation moved on, and he fielded questions about his show and travels. Leigh always gathered an interesting crowd, and he asked about the others' latest projects and successes with genuine interest. Gallery exhibitions, book launches, a prestigious medical association award, a couple of needle-in-the-haystack stock picks.

There was more, but he didn't catch the rest because after a while his mind got caught in a loop.

Octavia. Octavia. It was not a common name. Normally he wouldn't have given it a second thought, but that was a weird, gossipy conversation—and it was about Quinn.

Why the hell did he know the name Octavia?

Leigh retreated to the kitchen again. When she returned this time, she set a gorgeous cake and heaping bowl of fresh, cut fruit at each end of the table. He watched absent-mindedly as the realization hit him.

Octavia's. If his mind wasn't playing tricks on him, it was some kind of S&M place, a club.

She was going to a kink club? Not Quinn.

Pull my hair. Slap my face.

He had been so careful with her. Would others be?

He reached into his breast pocket, took out his phone nonchalantly, and unlocked it, hoping no one would notice.

Leigh did, a disapproving or perhaps insulted eyebrow subtly rising.

"I'm really sorry—my producer is still at the office and in a bind. I need to answer a text."

Although he had sworn he would not lie again after lying his ass off to Delphine, tonight he made an exception. His fingers tapped out "Octavia's" in the browser search bar.

Sure enough, Octavia's was a dungeon, a BDSM club.

He recalled the night he now thought of as their turning point, the night she leaned against him. How, earlier that evening, she had continued to ask for more and more strikes from the slapper, how she could hardly stand after the full-tilt speed of the vibrator, how she lay blindfolded and spread-eagled in front of him as he dripped melting ice over her breasts, how the inside of her pussy felt when she was about to come.

He thought of how other nights he had ended their play because it seemed like too much sensation, too much pain.

He stood and pushed in his chair. The surrounding conversations dropped to a lull as everyone looked up. "I hope you'll all excuse me—my producer ran into a snag with the next episode, and I need to give him a hand at the office. It's been a pleasure."

He went around to Leigh and kissed her on both cheeks, French style. "I'm sorry to eat and run," he offered lamely.

"Duty calls. I'm glad you could make it."

"Thanks for understanding." He hadn't pulled it often, but on those few occasions when he needed an out, no one argued with a two-cheeked kiss or an urgent, if imaginary, text from his producer.

"When Quinn returns my calls again, I'll let her know you asked for her."

Oh, I'm definitely asking for her.

He pictured some expressionless, burly bouncer outside Octavia's that he would somehow have to bypass to get to her. "Please do."

Really, he should stay away, leave well enough alone. The other shoe he always worried about had dropped. She had ghosted him; their whatever it had been was over.

So why was he jogging down the street toward Octavia's to look for her?

While waiting at a crosswalk, he confirmed the address on his phone. He had no idea if she would be there, but he had to check. The thought of her at some kind of dungeon—

vulnerable, alone, asking other men to do what she had asked him to do . . .

Shit. He hissed under his breath as he looked at the web page. The bold type, he hadn't noticed that earlier.

At the other side of the intersection, he moved out of the flow of humanity and paused to fill in a fake name and other details so he could score the golden ticket or secret code or whatever the fuck he needed to get in. But at least they were making some attempt at security.

He shook his head as if to dislodge the jealous thoughts. It was not only jealousy; he felt protective of her. He'd felt that way since that very first night when he laid eyes on her coming out of the kitchen, clutching a glass of red wine so tightly he worried it might shatter in her hand.

The feelings that arose in him that evening, they were hard to put words to, but he had been in—and screwed up—enough relationships to know that some whys were impossible to explain.

One thing he knew was that seeing her, thinking about her, gave him the strangest, warmest, most wonderfully disorienting feeling in his chest. And that ignited an overpowering urge to take care of her, to protect her, to please her, in spite—or maybe because—of her obvious strength.

She would not be pleased with him tonight.

He hoofed it closer and closer to Octavia's, his temples pounding with each step. Not only not pleased. Royally pissed for invading her privacy was probably more like it.

His boss would be royally pissed too if some dickwad recognized him and posted a photo of him in a sex-club-dungeon-whatever-the-fuck-you-called-it on social media.

This is a bad idea.

But clips of her continued to play behind his eyes, like edited scenes coming together into a cohesive storyline:

undressing in front of him that first time, bent over the arm of the couch, blindfolded and bound. Her skin damp with sweat. The weight of her body leaning into him, so close he could inhale the scent of her hair, raspberries and a hint of vanilla.

It was more than physical for him. More than magnetic attraction and intense sex. She had turned to him. She had trusted him with so much—her safety, her need—and revealed to him her desire. She had surrendered something magnificent to him: herself.

He had no choice but to see if she was—he recalled the women at Leigh's, throat clearing instead of making air quotes—visiting Octavia.

He checked the phone again. The map recalibrated and zoomed in, the blue dot throbbing like the pulse in his temple.

When he looked up, he saw the small swirly silver sign on the lamppost. It reminded him of Paris. It could have marked an eleventh arrondissement patisserie or an upscale boutique.

He tapped the "I'm here" button in the app as he cased the place. Wine-colored curtains obscured the windows, so there was no peering in to see if he could spot her. But at least no burly, cranky bouncer tried to stop him from opening the door.

9

WORDLESS NEED

The metal restraints—fast cuffs, Octavia called them—were cold against her wrists. She concentrated on the contrast. Hot drops of wax fell on her back from the wick of the candle in Octavia's hand. The wax cooled so fast, each molten droplet plunking onto her back, then hardening, tightening her skin, a minute pinch. Tonight, like the other nights during the past two weeks she had been coming to the club, she savored the feeling, let her attention meld with sensation.

It had the desired effect.

Subspace. Octavia had explained it simply, capturing the ethereal in a single word, and allowed Quinn to float in it.

If she were still and quiet enough, attentive enough, she could almost identify the bend in time when the loosening began, the sudden onset of lightness, the shift to an altered state.

She needed this badly tonight. Correction: She had needed this badly since she sent Jonathan away two weeks ago.

That day had been horrible, a low point worse than she had experienced in a long time.

Until Harris died, she had assumed grief was like recovering after an illness, lessening little by little, day by day, until you were healed. No, not healed, but functional. Able to sleep a few hours at night. Able to wake without having cried in your dreams. Able, perhaps reluctantly willing, to glance into the not-too-distant future.

It was nothing like that. Grief's MO was to ambush at random places and times, sneak attacks, light-footed but brutal.

It came and went whenever it fucking pleased, occasionally even more cruel now than right after it happened.

It snuck onto her doorstep that day a couple of weeks ago in the guise of those boxes of laundered shirts from Harris's old dry cleaner. Shirts that would not be worn again, lying still in boxes stapled with a yellow carbon-copy slip that listed one by one the phone calls he didn't answer.

Those were the ways grief played you: sudden, mundane, crippling.

That night, with Jonathan, she couldn't keep the feelings at bay. She needed to hurt to distract from them. She had asked him to slap her face, and in trying to do something gentler and less jarring, like jerking a fistful of her hair, he accidentally broke the necklace.

She was positive once she saw the chain, with its twisted links wrenched from the pendant, fallen next to her on the bed that heartache and guilt would crush her then and there. She hadn't deserved the necklace and—like her marriage to Harris, like his last days she had not cherished enough—she had let it break.

And once it was broken, the chain and interlocking hearts that had been a posthumous gift morphed into a mirror, a mirror that reflected her carelessness as a wife and, now, her failure as a widow.

She had not seen Jonathan since. She had let his calls go to voice mail. She had let his texts stack up unanswered.

And she hated that she missed him.

How could she grieve for one man while she craved another? Craved the way he would reach for her before he had even taken off his shoes. Craved how he understood her wordless need. Craved how she could turn her body over to him silently, secretly, entirely.

And yet.

His touch, his ability to read her, his tenderness while delivering wave after wave of sensation, his hesitance to hit her—it all left her feeling too close, too exposed.

The necklace underscored that vulnerability; it reflected her betrayal, her giving her body and thoughts and desire to someone else. It reflected a fact she could no longer ignore: Jonathan was no longer enough of a stranger.

At Octavia's, no one could tell what she needed simply by looking at her, by touching her, by knowing her, although wasn't knowing impossible after such a short time? But still, somehow, he did.

That's why, when Octavia had called with an invitation to join the club, she accepted and became an official member. Because sensation, sometimes pain, at the club for her they had little to do with sex or exposure, intimacy or betrayal. Here, in the safety of Octavia's, unlike with Jonathan, her need was low risk.

She had come back to Octavia's several times since her last night with him, each time meeting other members as they hung their everyday, outside-world things in individual wardrobes in the changing areas.

Out on the main floor, she would drift among the

singles, couples, and groups, awkwardly introducing herself and attempting small talk until the others wandered off with their playmates. But as soon as she would start to feel lost, Octavia seemed to find her, and they would head to one of the unoccupied alcoves.

Octavia would massage her upper back with oil first, then slowly drip the wax, starting just under the narrow fabric band at the neck of the backless dress she had dug out of the back of her closet.

Sometimes Octavia would alternate the wax with lashes from a flogger, a rhythm that enveloped her, spun her until she was drifting and lost.

Tonight, the warm wax and the whoosh of the suede tails unleashed a heat that radiated throughout her body. She listened closely for the faintest hiss as drops from the candle fell to her skin.

This, the club, was a new world to her, one she wanted to spend more time in. She didn't understand it yet—its myriad kinks and fetishes, or her own desires.

But she did understand acceptance, and she felt that here in spades. Her need didn't require explanation. Octavia's club had become a refuge; it offered relief. Her senses were heightened here, eclipsing the thoughts, the emotions, the guilt.

As Octavia continued with the wax and the flogger, Quinn melted into the warmth, imagined it spiriting her body away.

The heat and sting stopped suddenly. Her head felt heavy as she lifted it and craned her neck to see why. In a brief, beautiful moment of silence before the storm, she could actually hear the wax crack as she moved.

"OCTAVIA, WE HAVE A SITUATION—" someone yelled from the front of the club. Alex? His voice grew louder. "Stop. You can't just go in . . ."

"Five minutes," a man growled.

That voice she knew. She dropped her forehead onto the table. Fucking hell.

Octavia bent closer to her ear. "You know him, I take it? Should I call for help?"

"No, it's okay. Can you"—she tugged at the restraints— "undo me?"

Jonathan came to a stop by the alcove's archway. Alex caught up to him. "Hey man, you can't do this. There's a process, and we need ID."

Alex's hand closed around Jonathan's upper arm, and he shrugged it away.

"I said I need five minutes."

"I know him," Quinn said, "and he won't even be five minutes." She climbed off the table and adjusted her dress as she went toward him, embarrassment heating her face.

The last thing she wanted was a public spectacle like this. She had heard it over and over the past couple of weeks, how important it was not to disrupt other members' scenes.

Jonathan stared at her, then pulled one of her shoulders forward to peek around at her back. She pictured the criss-crossed lines of wax and avoided his face so she wouldn't see his reaction.

"What are you *doing*?" he demanded.

Her jaw clenched; her hands balled into fists. "Let's go outside."

She slunk past Octavia. "I'm so sorry. I'll be right back."

Alex was shaking his head as she led Jonathan toward

the door. "Not cool, man. It's members only and there's a procedure to follow. So not cool."

The dreamy music inside gave way to the sounds of the street outside—taxis honking, blurred conversations as people hurried by, sirens wailing in the distance, their sound making her heart race and her stomach turn.

They stood facing each other in the June heat.

"How dare you!" she spat at him.

"I was worried," he said, his voice low and raspy. "What are you *doing* here?"

"You have some nerve."

"I don't get it, Quinn. You cut me off, but you'll come to a sex club with total strangers, where people don't give a rat's ass about you or what you're going through?" He brought his hand to the top of his head and blew a breath hard out his mouth.

"Okay, number one: It's not a *sex* club. And they may not give a damn about my personal issues, but they don't want anything from me either."

"Oh, yeah. I've demanded sooo much from you. I get it. I care, and that scares the hell out of you, doesn't it?"

"You know," she said, ignoring his question, pointing back and forth angrily between them, "This isn't a Thing. Between us. It's not a relationship. I had one of those—for twenty years. It vanished." She snapped her fingers mid-air. "And so did half of myself. So you'll have to forgive me for not wanting to kiss or cuddle or to hold your fucking hand. Besides, you of *all* people are not relationship material."

He backed up, blinking in surprise. "You're right. But even if I were, I wouldn't want you to have to hold my fucking hand."

And then he turned and walked off.

She watched his back, but he didn't turn around. Some part of her wanted him to see her going back into the club, wanted to hurt him more than she already had with her words.

Because somehow it seemed safer for hurt and anger to grow between them than the other feelings she was fighting.

Alex was near the desk when she re-entered. "Everything okay?"

"Yeah. I'm so sorry about that."

"No problem. We were keeping an eye on you." He tipped his head toward the closed-circuit monitor with its view of the now empty sidewalk outside.

"Thanks. Is Octavia still around?"

"She went up to her office to take a quick call. She said she would be right down, but let me text her . . ."

"No, no, that's okay. I just wanted to apologize. Can you tell her for me?"

"Sure thing," Alex said, turning to his phone, which was buzzing like mad. He read a text and looked up, barely. "I gotta go—the winch isn't working right. Someone could get hurt."

Last time she was here, a man had been suspended from the ceiling in a cage. She appreciated Alex's worry about the winch.

As he headed toward the open space, he turned back. "I'll tell her for you as soon as I'm done fixing it. Don't worry. Seriously, it's all good."

She nodded awkwardly, tried to smile. As she raised her hand to give him a small wave, the wax pinched.

In the dressing room bathroom, she twisted around to see her back in the mirror and picked it off, chunk by chunk. Jonathan had ruined this for her.

On top of wrenching the necklace and following her here—because how else could he have found her?—he had ruined *this*; he had ruined her escape.

She left the club through the dressing room exit, emerging from the second door under the building's tall, wide staircase.

It hadn't occurred to her to ask him how he'd found her, but there really couldn't be any other explanation—he must have been out, caught sight of her walking from the train, and followed her uptown. She shook her head as she turned toward Penn Station.

The air was still and heavy as she walked, but a feathery sensation tickled her with an eerie chill, and goose bumps rose on her arms.

He approached from the shadows cast by the tall staircase of a neighboring building and blocked her path.

Damn it, why couldn't he just leave her *alone*?

Her fists clenched again, and she looked up—

It wasn't him.

THIS MAN'S voice was dry and cold like a high-desert night. "Leaving already?"

She ignored him and swerved toward the curb to widen the distance between them. He stepped sideways toward her, close enough to smell—something medicinal, unpleasantly piney.

Close enough for her not to be fooled by the expensive cut of his suit, which didn't soften the sharp, severe lines of his face. Or his twisted smirk. Nicely dressed or not, he gave her the creeps.

If she were on the other side of Octavia's door, a similar sensation of tingling down her neck, of unease speeding down her back, might have intrigued her. On the other side of Octavia's door, there was consent and protocol. There were limits and rules. There was closed-circuit TV and staff monitors to make sure no one got hurt.

On the other side of Octavia's door, it was safe, like a wild amusement park ride, thrilling but controlled.

But they were not on the other side of Octavia's door, they were outside, alone on a dark city street, no longer in front of the club's doorway with the hidden camera.

The dryness of her mouth, the rubberiness in her legs, the rush and pounding of her heartbeat in her ears—they all told her to get away.

She pulled her purse closer to her body and took off. No way she was pausing to kick off her heels. One flew off soon enough, but the other stayed firmly in place. The disparity threw off her gait, and she hiked up her dress so she could lengthen her stride.

And then that heel that wouldn't leave her foot was stuck in something on the ground and like a dream in slow motion she couldn't move her leg no matter how hard she tried. She heard the thud and rattle as her head hit metal, tasted iron in her mouth, saw her own legs not underneath her but aloft.

Something unyielding and cold pressed against her cheekbone.

He hovered over her, watching, two of him side by side, both of his mouths laughing.

Sick asshole.

She got on all fours, scrambled off the metal subway grate, and tried to focus her vision. She was almost at the intersection. If she could get to her feet and run, maybe there was an open shop or a restaurant up ahead or . . .

If she could get to her feet.

Her head weighed a ton, but she lifted it. Thank goodness, he was walking away, slowly—sauntering, the prick—fading into the night. She stood and leaned back against a tree by the curb to catch her breath.

The sound of footsteps made her turn. Alex and Octavia rushed toward her. She didn't like the look on their faces.

"You okay?" Alex asked as he got close. "Why don't you sit down?"

He caught up to her and helped her down. Quickly, he took off his black t-shirt, gathered it, and held it against her cheek. His hand quivered. "Did he hurt you?"

"I fell. I'm okay. I'm okay." The second time, she said it more to herself than to him.

Octavia spoke into her phone, giving their location, holding Quinn's wayward shoe in her other hand.

She motioned toward Octavia's phone. "Really, I'm fine. I just need to sit for a second."

"You should get checked out," Alex said. "Looks like you landed hard, and you might need a couple of stitches." He jutted his chin toward her cheek.

"How did you know I was out here?"

"I met Octavia on the floor and gave her your message while we walked back to the front desk. When we got there, we both noticed some motion on the monitor at the edge of the frame. She looked at me, and I looked at her. It's been a weird night—not only because of your . . . friend. The vibe was off, so we came out just to check. And here we are."

He sat cross-legged beside her. Octavia was um-hmm'ing into the phone while watching her, and Quinn gestured with both hands, palms down. *You can hang up; I'm okay.*

Octavia didn't hang up, and soon police sirens wailed, and the air began to flash red and blue.

Quinn's stomach lurched. The last time she saw those kinds of lights, they were outside her cabin at Hollinger, her idyllic spot in the woods where, until then, nothing bad seemed able to happen. She had gone to the door at the sound of the car, unusual on the colony's grounds. The loudest noise was usually a staff member dropping off a lunch basket or another writer cracking a twig as they hiked on the nearby path. Two officers had emerged from underneath the lights and asked if she was Quinn Layborn.

Yesss?

Do you know a Harris Layborn?

He's my husband.

There's been an accident.

Where is he? Take me to him.

Ma'am . . . The one talking paused just a little too long to take off his hat, like in tear-jerker movies neither she nor Harris liked. Only this one was real. The officer's mouth continued to move, but her wails drowned out the rest of his words.

Alex brushed her arm as he stood up, bringing her back to the present. Doors slammed, and an EMT knelt to check her out.

An officer took a report and told the three of them what Quinn already knew from having married an attorney-turned-judge. Asking a question, smirking, creeping her out wasn't a crime.

Still, he assured them the local precinct would step up

patrols on the block. And she had Harris's old contacts she could call, although that would require explaining what she had been doing here.

When they were done, the EMT helped her up, steadying her with a hand on her shoulder and elbow as they walked to the waiting gurney.

"I'll go with her," Octavia told him.

As she climbed into the back of the ambulance after Quinn, Octavia teased in a furtive whisper, "You don't have a medical fetish, do you?"

Quinn appreciated the attempt at levity. "Not that I was aware of, but now I kind of wish I did."

Octavia laughed, her smile instantly soothing, and sat on the bench beside the gurney. She scraped off an overlooked piece of wax from Quinn's collarbone as one of the EMTs closed the doors.

In the emergency room, round after round of nurses and residents in various specialties asked her the same litany of questions.

When they were done, a woman came into the bay, drawing the curtain behind her. She introduced herself as a social worker.

"Who else can I call for you, Mrs. Layborn?" she asked after another battery of questions. She kept a disdainful eye trained on Octavia, who was dressed like, well, the owner of Octavia's.

"No one," Quinn answered. Leigh was not an option.

"Well, you let me know if you change your mind. I'll check back with you later." She patted Quinn's shoulder condescendingly and cast another disapproving glance in Octavia's direction before pulling the curtain open to leave. So much for social work.

"I'll go so I don't raise more eyebrows and embarrass you—I didn't have time to change, I'm sorry. But one thing before I go—I've set up a meeting first thing tomorrow to review our security system and policies. I feel terrible about this—we've never had trouble before. Safety is so important to us, and then . . . this." She shook her head ruefully.

"It's okay. It wasn't your fault." Quinn reached out and touched her forearm. "Would you mind staying for a bit?" Octavia was anything but embarrassing. She was strong and caring, a calming, welcome presence.

"Not at all. I'll stay as long as you want. But I really think . . ." They both listened as the noise level rose on the other side of the curtain. Quinn braced herself for a group of med students to tromp in and gawk, as if she were a test tube specimen.

Not medical students—she was definitely wrong about that.

Alex came in first, followed by a bunch of people she had seen at the club tonight, some dressed in everyday clothes, some in slinky black tops and pants and skirts and kinky boots.

She lost track of how many streamed in and surrounded her on the gurney. The people she hadn't met introduced themselves; the ones within arm's reach stretched to shake or squeeze her hand. Those further away gave her knee or her shin a friendly jostle.

Preet, a member she had met a few nights ago, spoke up. "If you're comfortable giving us your number, we'll each text you ours. You *always* have people to hang out with at the club—to play with or just to *be*." She closed her eyes and made a chill, meditative gesture with her hands that made Quinn giggle. "We can meet up and go together or walk you to Penn Station when you leave—you never have to be alone at Octavia's. Not unless you want to be."

She gave the group her number and thanked them, again squeezing the hands of those she could reach just as the nurse came back with an orderly. His eyes widened at the crowd in the tiny space.

Preet held up her phone and shook it—*we'll be in touch* —and the group, except for Octavia, shuffled out of the bay.

"Someone is *very* popular," the nurse said, "and now it's time for your MRI. By the time you're done, the plastic surgeon should be here. We'll get you all stitched up, good as new, and into a room for the night, for observation."

The orderly was about to release the brake with his foot, but Quinn stopped him. "Could you give me a minute?"

"Sure, but they're waiting for you down in Radiology, and it's a busy night."

"I know, just a second, thanks." She held up her index finger to show she'd be fast and looked toward Octavia. "Can I use your phone to send a quick text? Mine's . . . hopefully around here somewhere." She had it with her in the ambulance, so it must be with her clothes and shoes.

Octavia gave her a funny smile and handed Quinn her phone.

She tapped out her text and passed it back. "Why are you looking at me like that?"

"I'm glad you're reaching out to him. I'm not condoning what he did or asking any questions. But there was a lot of emotion between you two."

"Yeah. There's more there than I want to admit. It feels a little . . . complicated."

"Ready?" the orderly asked.

"Ready." As they began to move, she remembered Octavia's unfinished sentence a moment ago and turned toward her. "Hey, what were you going to say before everyone came in—'But I really think . . .'"

A knowing grin broke out on Octavia's usually serene face. "I was going to say, But I really think you should get in touch with him."

10

NO REASON TO LIE

"You can see her now," the guy at the nurses' station told him. "Third door on the right."

Jonathan was practically at Quinn's room by the time the man finished the sentence, although he paused for a second in the open doorway, hands in his pockets. Her brief text said she was fine, but he needed to prepare himself in case she wasn't.

She looked up at him, then immediately dropped her gaze. The eye above the bandage on her cheek was surrounded by black and blue, and a few spots of dried blood flecked her puffy lower lip. Octavia—or at least he assumed the woman who had been dripping hot wax on Quinn's body at the club earlier was Octavia—stood beside her.

"Hey," he said, not sure what kind of greeting was in order after she had ripped him a new one at the club but then texted him she was sorry and in the ER, could they talk?

"Hey. You came."

He went to the bed and stood across from Octavia. "Of

course I came. Did you really think I wouldn't?"

"I wouldn't blame you. I owe you a big apol—"

"So I should get back to the club," Octavia interjected, gesturing toward the door.

Quickly, she took hold of Quinn's forearm with both her hands. "I'll check on you in the morning. If you need anything tonight, call me. Any time. I'll get your number once I'm back at the club and text you mine." She hurried out before Quinn could answer.

He held onto the bed rail to keep from touching her. She had spoken the brutal truth outside the club—she didn't want anything more than a fuck buddy, and he wasn't in a position to offer more, anyway. He might have caught himself falling for her these past weeks, but she was right. He was *not* relationship material.

A nauseating realization had hit him as he walked home from Octavia's earlier, that the fact he was a cheater was actually why she had chosen him that first night, that to her he was just the type of guy for a one-time fuck.

He had been right to think each time she texted him would be the last; he was lucky it took as long as it did to end. He had only come here because it was Quinn, and she had reached out to him. And he could not stop caring about her, or stop wanting to protect her, so easily.

The ache in his chest throbbed; it wasn't easy to be near her now, knowing their arrangement was over. "You don't look so fine. What happened?"

"I fell." She stopped worrying the edge of the thin white blanket and looked at him. "How did you know I was there, at Octavia's?"

"May I?" he asked, pointing toward the side of the bed where the railing ended.

"Please." She shifted her legs over to make room for

him. He didn't want to answer her question. It didn't seem like the right time to tell her that her colleagues at Leigh's had been gossiping.

"How'd you fall?"

"I was running, and I tripped."

Why would she be running?

"Sorry to interrupt." It was the nurse who had been at the station when Jonathan arrived. He came into the room holding out a white plastic bag with blue capital letters. PATIENT BELONGINGS. "The ER sent up your things," he told Quinn.

Between the N and the G, a pointy black patent heel poked through the bag.

Now it was making sense.

Jonathan's temple now throbbed along with the ache in his chest as he pictured her in those heels, pictured what he had done to her in those heels.

He sprang to his feet, anger like a tight metal coil inside him. "You tripped? Or you went back inside the club after I left and found someone to knock you around how you wanted?"

Her eyes widened, the tears instantaneous. So was his regret.

That was cruel. It was easy to lash out; he felt stupid. Since seeing her at the club, he kept thinking what an amateur he was, mustering all his nerve to pull her hair or slap her ass and do her at the same time. He remembered his excitement as he scrolled around the kink shop website, clicking toys into his cart, when she apparently was far more hardcore.

Geez, he had been nervous about tying the fucking silk scarves too tight. What a clown.

"That wasn't fair. I'm sorry." He reached to pull a tissue

from the box on the nightstand and handed it to her. "But at least tell me the truth. We have no reason to lie to each other."

She dabbed the tissue between her eye and the bandage. "I'm not lying to you. I tripped outside. When I left . . . Some guy . . . I thought . . ." She began gulping for air between the fragments.

He touched her shoulder and tried to soothe her through the gown. Did the asshole hurt her? Did he put a hand on her? Jonathan needed to know. But this was about her, not him, and he bit the inside of his lip to keep his mouth shut until she finished.

"Some guy approached me outside. I got a bad feeling, and I ran. Stupid heels." She glanced at the bag the nurse had set on the bedside table. "When I fell, he laughed and walked away."

He wiped a falling tear with his thumb as she continued. "Octavia and the club monitor saw something on the security footage and they came outside to see if anything was going on. The people at the club aren't some dangerous sex-crazed maniacs like you seem to think."

"No, no, no, you're right. I don't think that at all, and I was way out of line showing up there tonight and with what I just said—it was insensitive and wrong and I'm sorry."

Her gaze remained on the ceiling, not on him.

"I have to ask you something. *Why?* I get that different sensations—pain, even—can feel good, erotic. And I get that hurting physically might distract you from the emotional stuff. But that night with me, when you wanted me to hit your face, that part I don't understand."

Her chin quivered, and her eyes welled again. He tugged at the bed rail until it released and, careful not to jostle her, he climbed in beside her and placed his palm on her chest, hoping the touch, the pressure, would soothe her.

No matter what the future held for them, if anything at all, it killed him to see her distraught.

"Talk to me," he whispered. "Please?"

She sniffed and wiped away more tears.

He turned further toward her, until his forehead touched hers, until there was hardly a hair's width of space between them—their own little bubble. "Help me understand."

She kept her eyes closed while she spoke. "I don't know how to stop feeling guilty. I know it wasn't my fault, not directly, but if I had done things differently, it might not have happened. That sick feeling,"—she touched her stomach—"it won't go away.

"And then I have sex with someone else . . . you. The only way I could justify it was to focus on the pain. If it hurt, then I wasn't such an awful wife. Widow. That's why I couldn't talk to you. I hated myself for what I was doing. It felt like I was cheating. But I couldn't stop. Without talking, with the pain, I could almost pretend I was someplace else."

She sniffled again and dabbed her cheek with the tissue. "It started to feel so good, like so much pressure finally releasing. Like having a nightmare, running away from something, and then suddenly you see a safe place to hide, and you feel this huge . . . relief. It spun into a cycle—the more I wanted, the guiltier I felt, which made me want to hurt even more."

"Back up for a second. What wasn't your fault?"

She moved her head away from his and looked down at her hands, toying with the base of her ring finger, as if her wedding band were still there. "The accident. He was coming to see me." A tear dripped onto the white pillowcase.

He remembered now. Leigh had told him, and it had been in all the articles. She had won some award, a fellowship, to attend an artist colony upstate, and she was away from home when Harris was involved in a terrible car crash.

"Jesus, Quinn. It was not your fault. How could you think that?"

"I left without saying goodbye. We were supposed to have dinner together the night before I was scheduled to leave. I finished packing early, I'd finished all the errands I had to do, and I decided to leave that afternoon instead. He was still in court, so I left a voice mail to tell him I was going early. A voice mail."

"I'm sure it thrilled him you got the fellowship, and he must have understood you wanted to get up there to write."

"He called me back just as I was putting my stuff in the car. He asked if I could stay, if I could drive up in the morning as planned so we could keep our dinner date. I insisted I wanted to get going, and I hate myself for that—I was selfish. I put writing first, before my husband. We could have had another night together."

She wiped more tears away with the heel of her hand, and his heart felt about to split in half seeing the pain in her eyes. He rubbed her chest.

"And like always, he didn't get angry. He teased me and said I owed him a date. That's why he was driving up the next weekend. That Saturday morning, we talked for a few minutes on the phone and he asked what we were having for dinner. I was short with him, gave him a snappish answer because I wanted to get back to work—why were we wasting time talking about that? I told him I loved him before I hung up, but fast, not like I usually did, not like I meant it, and I ended the call before he could say it back. I didn't realize he was dropping a hint about driving up for dinner."

"I'm sorry. So sorry," was all Jonathan said.

"That was the last time we talked. The police filled in the rest. His overnight bag was in the car; the GPS was programmed to Hollinger. There was a jewelry box in his pocket . . ."

Oh, for fucking fuck's sake, Jonathan would bet his last dollar—no, his life—that he knew what was in the box.

The heart necklace.

Of any object in that huge fucking haunted house of hers, he had to break the single most precious thing she had left.

"It wasn't your fault," he said. "Look at me." He took her face in his hand and stroked her good cheek with his thumb.

"He planned to surprise me, and I hung up on him. If I hadn't left early, if I hadn't broken our plans, he wouldn't have been on that highway that day. Because of what I did, he's gone. And I never got to say goodbye."

He held a tissue to her cheek to keep the tears from wetting her bandage and put his other arm under her shoulders to bring her closer. "These things aren't in our control."

Now he got why she couldn't write.

It wasn't just the loss, but also the suddenness of it and the guilt about the chain of events. "It was *not* your fault." He pulled back to look at her. "You have to accept that. You cannot carry something like that. You know he wouldn't want you to."

"We didn't say goodbye. Because I didn't let us. I'm not

sure how to get past that. It's so cliché, but I wish I could do things over. I wish I had one more chance."

"He knew how much you loved him. One terse phone call didn't change that. I remember how you two were when he visited you on the movie set. We all saw how loving you were with each other." He let go of her shoulders. "Can I tell you something?"

She turned toward him.

"Seeing how in love you two were made me realize what was missing in my marriage. It made me feel lonely and hopeless, like there was no way out, and I knew then, unequivocally, I'd made a big mistake."

"Gee, what an inspiration."

"But it was. Your relationship opened my eyes to a problem I hadn't been able or willing or brave enough to admit. I handled it all wrong—I cheated instead of asking for a divorce—which was spineless, cowardly. But seeing what a marriage could be like between two people who were head over heels in love, even after many years, made me realize what was lacking in mine. Caring and friendship, yes, a lot. But what you and Harris had? Uh-uh. Light years away."

"I'm sorry you didn't experience that. It's wonderful when it happens."

"I can imagine." *Especially with you.* "You two had something truly special. I'm just sorry . . ."

She stopped him with her finger to his lips, as she had their first night together. Time for him to back off.

He wanted to be there for her, to comfort her, whatever that meant. Although it probably, unfortunately, meant no more rough-and-tumble sex.

Or any sex, for that matter. A year—thirteen, fourteen

months, whatever—really was nothing. While her publisher and Leigh eyed the calendar like it was time to flip the page, she was only starting the grueling process of rebuilding her life.

If he wanted to be part of it, he would need to give her space and time to work through things however she needed to. He would not ask her how she saw their future. He would not ask her not to go to Octavia's.

If he held onto their relationship too tightly, she would slip like water through his clenched fist.

Her eyes had closed and soon her neck relaxed against his hand. Her chest slowly rose and fell in sleep. As much as he would miss having sex with her, he would gladly take this in its place.

Maybe over time he would get to witness other intimate moments—how she cocked her head to put on an earring, how she sang in the shower, how she stretched before she got out of bed in the morning.

He pressed his lips lightly to her head, releasing a hint of raspberry scent that made his heart soft and his cock hard, although not necessarily in that order.

It's a hospital. Have some fucking manners.

HE HELD her while she slept, until a new nurse came into the room. He raised a finger to his lips to signal Quinn was sleeping, but his movement woke her. "How are we feeling?" the nurse asked her as she approached the bed.

"Okay. Sore. But better," she said, putting her hand on his chest. He placed his over it, feeling instantly better too.

"You're going to be sore for a while," the nurse said, nodding. "How's the vision? Still double?"

"Not anymore. Just one of everything."

"One's good, we like one. We still want you to stay the rest of the night for observation, to rule out a concussion. I'll come back in a couple of hours to check on you. Your friend can stay if he doesn't mind a backache tomorrow." She nodded toward the aging blue pleather recliner in the corner.

"Would you be more comfortable if I move to the chair?" he asked Quinn once they were alone again.

"No, stay here." She closed her fingers around his hand and looked him in the eye. "I am sorry for what I said outside Octavia's. I don't know what this is between us, but it's hardly nothing. You gave me something I needed but didn't feel entitled to. I felt safe with you; I knew I could trust you. I *know* I can trust you."

"That's an incredible gift."

He thought of how she had bared herself to him, chosen him, entrusted him with her pain and her desire. That was an amazing expression of trust—one he now began to think he might be deserving of after all.

"I was a little slow to figure out what you wanted, but soon I could tell. It was erotic as hell, even though I worried I might hurt you. But your expressions—relief, escape, maybe ecstasy, I hope. It was such a turn-on to do that for you. It was one of the most incredible experiences I've ever had, to watch you so closely for all these subtle cues—which muscles tensed and relaxed, how your skin changed texture, your wetness, the sounds you made . . ."

She uttered a nearly inaudible moan and squeezed his hand tighter.

And now his cock was uncomfortably straining against his fly, hearing more of her cries and gasps in his memory banks. "All those signs that told me when it was enough, or when to push you further . . ."

His fingertips caressed the back of her hand and the peaks and valleys of her knuckles. He could explore her body for days. "But I'm sorry, I couldn't hit you. Not in the face."

"It wasn't fair of me to ask. We never talked about limits, and I wasn't thinking about it from your point of view."

It was a need, an impulse, she had shared with him—if that wasn't a pure show of her trust, what was? And it meant everything.

He let go of her hand long enough to set the alarm on his phone for an hour. He had always heard you should check on people with a possible concussion every hour, not two, and he didn't want to take any chances with her. He would make his own hospital protocol.

She fell asleep against him and, when the alarm chimed, he watched her open her eyes. "How do you feel?"

"Same. Okay." She pulled the sheet around her hands and closed her eyes again.

"Wai . . . wait. Not so fast." He moved a piece of hair that had fallen onto her face. "Where are you?"

"Midtown Medical."

"What day is it?"

"Saturday. No, Sunday—it's after midnight."

"Good catch. Go back to sleep." He pressed his lips against the top of her head, but didn't kiss it.

In an hour, the nurse came in and roused her. When she left the room, he set his alarm for another hour.

"Do I have to open my eyes?" Quinn asked when it went off. He caught a tease of a smile, which he took as a good sign.

"You can keep them closed, but what novel of yours did we work on together?"

She smiled, but her hand flew to her cheek. It must hurt. "Oh, come on, too easy—*Market Day*."

When his phone sounded an hour later, she jumped in straightaway although her eyes remained closed. "My turn: What's the name of the owner of the stall that sold *imqaret* at the market in Birgu?"

He laughed. "Peter. You watched?"

The episode on Malta had run only once so far, last week, during that abyss in time when she wouldn't answer his texts or calls.

She nodded against him, sleepily. "I watched. I missed you."

They were both asleep when his phone dinged at six with a calendar alert. He fumbled for it and tapped the screen. Shit, where had his brain gone?

"What?" she asked.

"With everything last night, I wasn't thinking." He pictured the open suitcase on his bed. "I have to fly out again this afternoon."

Early morning light hadn't yet brightened the room, so maybe it was wishful thinking, but he could have sworn disappointment clouded her expression. "I can change it. I'll help you get settled at home and catch up with the team in a day or two."

"You are not. Where are you going?"

"Brazil, Argentina, and Chile."

"When do you come back?"

"This is a long one—almost three weeks."

She sighed. "Well, can we get together when you come home? I mean, not like that . . ." The blush rose in her cheeks as she stammered. "I know it might sound hypocritical. I practically take you hostage to have sex—a *lot* of sex—extraordinary sex . . ."

She glanced away, like she was picturing it. "And now I say I'm not ready for anything more, but . . ." She gazed up at him with those big brown eyes. "I'd still like to see you."

He took her hand again, and this time he laced his fingers between hers. "And I would like to see you. It doesn't sound hypocritical." He thought of that intense night, afterward on the floor, how she'd moved back toward him, almost close enough to spoon.

And last night, how she finally let him hold her, how she relaxed and fell asleep against him. How his chest felt so full when she did. "We can get together for whatever you want. Do you play chess?"

He loved her modest smile. "No. Scrabble."

"That's unfortunate," he teased. "I have a strict policy against playing that with writers. It's bad for my ego. How about this: I'll bring back spices from some of the markets, and I'll cook dinner for us. Saturday night, the . . ." He picked up his phone, opened his calendar, and gave her the date. "My place, on the terrace."

"That sounds perfect."

"It does. A lot better than having my ass handed to me on a wooden tile worth two points. Seven o'clock?"

"Seven o'clock."

That smile of hers, he would never tire of seeing it. He took both her hands and guided her back toward the stack of pillows.

"Rest. I'll check on you later." He held onto her until her weight shifted and her head touched the top pillow, releasing the scent of her hair.

If they were going to take a step back, he would have to

ask her to change her shampoo. The fucking raspberries were going to be his undoing.

Slowly, he stepped backward toward the door, facing her and watching as the vacant, faraway look in her eyes these past few weeks began to focus closer, he hoped, on the present.

11

ALMOST AS IF

The second she got home from the hospital, she took the orange bottle of pain medicine out of her purse, dropped the bag at the top of the stairs, and undressed on the way to the shower.

With her cheek out of the spray—plastic surgeon's orders—she let the warm water rain down, let the mist, the steam, soak into her skin.

When the pads of her fingers started to wrinkle, she turned the water off and pulled her towel from the rod. At the vanity, she pressed and twisted the cap off the pill bottle until it popped and eyed the capsules.

Her cheek was sore. Her body was bruised in a few spots and it hurt from hitting the ground, but she hadn't broken anything.

If she took the medicine, she would sleep, and she was tired. But the pain was not bad—it was nothing compared to the pain of despair she had felt all these months.

Or the outrage she felt at that creepy asshole the more she pictured his sneering face. The capsules would not help that, though. Tracking him down to learn if he had some connection to the club or one of its members would, and Harris had many a detective colleague. She placed the cap back on the bottle, twisted it until it clicked, and threw it into the trash.

She put on her robe and pulled the belt tighter, determined. People had told her she would know when it was time and, now, although she could not pinpoint exactly why, it was.

From the bedroom window, she looked out across the road to the ocean beyond. She would no longer let sorrow drown her. Instead, she would think of it like the unceasing rhythm of the waves, rolling in, surrounding her, and receding while she planted her heels and toes in the shifting sand to stay, more or less, in place until the cycle began again.

In the walk-in closet, she started with his suits, then his dress shirts, his work shoes and golf clothes, the old ripped jeans he kept around for house chores, the drawers of underwear and socks and winter pajamas.

When she got to the drawer with the soft, heathered t-shirts he used to wear on summer weekends, she took one out, unfolded it and brought it to her face, its texture against her cheek heartbreaking in its familiarity but the scent no longer of him.

She created a separate pile, *things to keep*.

The plastic surgeon had said not to lift anything heavy, so she carried his things downstairs in small batches and piled them near the back door.

The coat closet was next. His rain trench, his long wool winter coat, a ski jacket and pants, enough windbreakers to outfit a sailing team and, on the floor, the leather duffel he had packed to visit her, the one the police had recovered from the trunk and handed over to her.

She unzipped it and removed the contents—his boxers and white undershirts, a couple of casual t-shirts, the dress shirt he must have brought to wear to dinner.

"I'm so sorry," she whispered, the tears welling again.

After bringing everything to the stacks by the back door, she made a cup of tea and took it out to the garden. Peony bushes lined the stone path to the patio, cushions of moss brightening the spaces between the rocks.

She set the mug down and sat at their old teak table.

On summer mornings when he didn't have to be in court early, they would share coffee and breakfast before he went to his office and she went upstairs to hers. On Sundays they lingered over *The Times*.

She longed to smell the flowers' delicate aroma now, but the once-fragrant blossoms had withered; it was already late June.

Tears started down her cheeks again. He was just as excited as she was about the Hollinger Fellowship, and although he wanted to have dinner together, he would have understood why she left early and why she was short on the phone. That did not make her a terrible wife.

Harris knew her; he knew how intensely she wrote; he knew how intensely she loved him. One abrupt reaction on her part did not erase what they had shared for so long. Jonathan had voiced what deep down she already knew, but had trouble believing.

She would have to hold on to such fragments of certainty. Maybe these were all she would have, and they would have to be enough.

She would always regret leaving early, that she hadn't kept their dinner plans. She would always wish she had stayed on the phone longer that Saturday morning. She would always wish they had gotten to say goodbye.

But she would not continue to blame herself or let guilt drive her actions, define her existence.

The light was changing to the golden-green that heralds a heavy rain. The peony bushes rustled in the occasional gust. A few loose, wilted petals floated down to the flagstone, while others caught the breeze and flew.

The sleeves of her robe swayed, and the cooling air bristled the hair on her forearms. Something rustled behind her and she turned to see what it was, but nothing was there except the wind.

Between gusts, the humid air hung moist and heavy on her shoulders, almost as if hands were resting there.

Almost as if.

She touched her shoulder.

She had wished for this ever since it happened—not a vision of him in her dreams or her imagination or her memory, but to sense his presence.

She stayed still and quiet. A raindrop landed on the table. A few plinked the water in the birdbath. One alighted in the crook of her neck right near the spot where he used to kiss her.

"I love you," she whispered to the air, to him, to the place deep and safe in her heart where he would stay with her forever.

JONATHAN STOPPED at the apartment to finish packing and tied up last-minute logistics with Rich in a volley of texts.

On his way out, he took the painting down from the wall in the entry. Wasn't he on some level doing the same thing as Quinn? Continuing to blame himself by keeping it hanging there, a constant reminder of what he did wrong, of what he lost.

Unlike Quinn, though, losing Delphine *was* his fault.

He didn't know what he would do with the painting yet, so for now he set it against the back wall of the coat closet facing away from the doors. If things had ended differently between them, he might ask her if she wanted it, but there was no way. Like him, she would no longer see its beauty, only a reminder of their brokenness, of his infidelity.

He wanted to be whole for Quinn, and that would mean shutting off the voices in his head that continued to berate him for what he had done. Quinn's trust helped him see he didn't need the scarred painting to remind him how deeply he had betrayed a woman.

That dark, needy, cheating part of himself was just that, *part*. Not all of him. And knowing that meant he understood its power. From the depths of his soul, and with clear and utter certainty, he knew he would never do it again.

Maybe now he could finally forgive himself.

Gil texted he was waiting outside, and Jonathan took the elevator down to meet him. On the ride, they bantered about last night's baseball game, which he had mindlessly watched until Quinn texted from the hospital.

"Short detour, if you don't mind," he said, directing Gil to Delphine's shop, *De Paris Avec L'Amour*.

"I'll circle," Gil said when they were half a block away. There would be less than a snowball's chance in hell of finding a parking spot.

At the intersection, Jonathan hopped out and approached the wood-framed door underneath the black and white striped awning. *From Paris With Love*. A bell jangled as two women entered in front of him.

Inside, he paused and looked around. The first time he

had come here was shortly after she opened, after their split, and she was doing something in the back. An employee had gone to get her but came right back to tell him she was Very Busy. The poor guy smiled so awkwardly, Jonathan got the message and left.

The shop was just as full of charm today as back then, with the aged herringbone floor and creative displays of small-producer wines, like the ones from her family's vine-yard, and other imported specialties—squat cans of pâté de canard, oak barrels of olives, jars of cassoulet, bags of dried truffles, bars of fine soaps.

She curated an amazing inventory. Her picnic baskets—rented by the hour, day, or Hamptons weekend—were legendary. Customers only had to tell her how many people and if they had any requests or allergies, and she would fill the basket with delicacies paired with just the right wine.

If you didn't order by Monday afternoon, you couldn't get a basket for the following weekend. New Yorkers could be hard to please, but she had hit on an ingenious service that propelled the shop's success like rocket fuel.

He glanced across the narrow space, where a glass case by the register held shelves of croissants, pain au chocolat, and pastel macarons. Cheeses lived in a separate case on the other end of the shop to keep the strong smells away from the delicate baked goods.

A young woman worked behind the counter, making espresso for a couple seated at one of the two tiny bistro tables, all that fit in the brimming but small shop.

And there she was, coming out from the back, a big cellophane-wrapped basket blocking her view of him. He waited while she showed it to the customer and brought it to the register.

"Merci," the woman said. "Good luck. The entire neighborhood will miss your little touch of Pahr-ee—I wish you didn't have to close."

"That is very kind of you," Delphine replied in her flawless, slightly accented English. "It's for the best. I have missed France. But I will also miss New York."

The customer reached to hug her. As Delphine leaned in, she caught sight of him over the woman's shoulder. Her eyes closed as if shutting him out.

When the woman turned to leave, he approached Delphine, her black hair cut in a smartly shaggy bob, her green eyes narrowing at breakneck speed from surprise to scowl. "What are you doing here?"

"You're going back to France?"

Her look challenged. *Who wants to know?* "Yes. My father is not well."

"I'm sorry to hear that. How long will you stay?"

Her eyes rounded in that familiar way that told him he must not be getting it. "I'm leaving New York. I'm going *home* to France."

She looked around and lowered her voice. "I guess my father was right after all, wasn't he? New York turned out to be a mistake."

Jonathan was the mistake.

Against her father's judgment, he had convinced her to start a new life here, with him. Although her family ran the vineyard, she had her own career as a school administrator, and she found a similar job in the city.

Until something bright and shiny had crossed Jonathan's path.

His fuck-up not only cost their marriage, it cost her job at the chichi private school—"we need our staff to stay out of *any* fray," the principal had told him when, without telling Delphine, he had tried to intervene so she could keep her job.

That's when she had started the shop. And now she was giving it up to return home. It would be one more failure in her father's eyes and, far worse, her own.

"You didn't say why you're here. I'm busy."

"I . . . We . . . We never talked about it. It doesn't have to be right now, but shouldn't we?"

She looked at him like he had just stepped off a spaceship. "No, we shouldn't. I'm sure I've heard it already: You don't know what came over you. You wish things had turned out differently. You really loved me. You never meant to hurt me. Am I close?"

She didn't wait for his answer. "Save your empty words, Jonathan." She pronounced his name *zhu-na-ton* and, hearing it again, it felt like a punch to the solar plexus.

She was right; his words were worthless now. Thinking that talking about their breakup, about the affair, would give her the closure she hadn't asked him for now suddenly seemed condescending and self-centered. He was the one seeking closure; he wanted her forgiveness, but it was probably not forthcoming.

"Will you come back?" he asked. "You loved it here."

"I loved *you*. I loved New York because it made me think about life in a new country with you, about possibility. And now I'm closing my shop and going home. Alone. To sit by my father's sick bed. Does that answer your question?"

The bell above the door jangled behind him. "I have a customer." She looked past him dismissively. "Good bye, *Zhu-na-ton*."

FOR THE FIRST time in a long time, she had slept through the night.

Drawing the curtain back from the open window, she looked out. Wind rustled the dune grasses and stretched the clouds into feathery wisps like slow-motion salt-water taffy. Sun warmed the morning air. Birds chirped in the tree just outside the window and the surf crashed against the shore in the distance.

Maybe she would take a walk by the water later. How long since she had done that?

But first she went into her study. At the desk, she pulled out the marbled black and white notebook from Hollinger that she had stashed in the bottom drawer once she had gotten back home—her life, their life, indelibly changed.

As a little girl, she had loved those black and white notebooks, and she continued using them throughout her career for capturing ideas, brainstorming and exploration, rough outlines and sketches, early manuscript drafts.

She opened the cover and barely recognized the words inside; they could easily have belonged to someone else.

In many ways, she *was* someone else when she wrote them—curious, observant, optimistic, quick to laugh, a prolific writer, a happy wife.

She leafed through the pages, scanned the lines, tried to conjure the story she had been imagining, tried to remember what it was like to inhabit that place of flow where the ideas came and the sentences grew layer by layer until she had a paragraph, a page, a chapter, eventually a book.

Harris would share feedback on what she had written, on the themes and the characters and the plot twists. She smiled now, recalling how he would tease her about why, if she wanted another bestseller, she wrote no robots, vampires, or Vikings into her stories.

She closed the notebook and ran her hand over the smooth cover before putting it back in the drawer.

Phone in hand, she tapped the number from her list of contacts.

"You must have been reading my mind," Leigh said when she answered. "I've been wanting to call you, but," she hesitated, "you seemed to need a break from me."

"I'm sorry for running off and not being in touch. It's been . . . Well, you know how it's been."

"I'm sorry if I was pushing you too hard."

"That's why you're my friend, and why you get paid the big bucks," Quinn joked, trying to lighten the mood. "Would you have lunch with me, or dinner, whatever works with your schedule the day after tomorrow?"

She was hoping by then more of the bruising would lighten, at least enough that she could conceal the rest with makeup.

"Love to. I'm supposed to head out east Friday afternoon to meet Becca and Charles for the weekend. I'll leave early and we can have lunch near your neck of the woods."

"Perfect." It would be a hard conversation, but a necessary one. "Call me when you're on the road and we can decide where to meet."

"Will do. And I'll have to bring you up to speed on Becca's wedding plans—it's getting close."

"I can't wait to hear all about it. She must be so happy. I'm so happy *for* her."

Leigh's daughter was the real deal—independent, smart, kind, funny. While Leigh sometimes misread, or glossed over, emotional situations, Becca usually had an accurate read on things. In fact, the day of Leigh's "small" dinner party, Becca had left Quinn a message saying she wouldn't be there. "I know this isn't your scene—I'll come see you another time. Stay strong."

Quinn heard the "My mom's at it again" between the lines, and it had touched her. She couldn't wait to meet the man Becca had been dating and now planned to share her life with.

Two days later, Quinn and Leigh agreed to meet at a cute little restaurant on the sleepy side street off the hamlet's main downtown strip. The place was popular with locals, a refuge on busy summer weekends.

In the parking lot, Leigh came over as Quinn got out of the car. "I was so glad you called," she said, reaching out for a hug.

Quinn relaxed into her embrace, then stepped back and put her hands on Leigh's shoulders to look at her. "I'm glad I called, too."

They walked the cobblestoned path to the entrance of the bright yellow saltbox cottage with its lime green trim, the flower boxes bursting with geraniums.

The screen door creaked shut behind them. Without thinking, Quinn lifted her sunglasses onto her head. Leigh gasped and grabbed her shoulder. "What *happened*?"

Quinn moved the glasses back down to the bridge of her nose, where she had meant to keep them. "My heel got caught in a sidewalk grate in the city and I fell."

"When did this happen?" Leigh asked, sizing up the side of her face, leaning back to take her in, evaluating and assessing.

"Last weekend. No concussion, only a few stitches. Not a big deal," she added, trying to shake Leigh's stare. No need to get into details.

"Well, it looks like a big deal. I wish you would have called me."

"I did," she said, smiling. "Just not immediately after it happened. I'm okay, really. Let's have lunch."

They were shown to a table and listened to the day's specials. When their server returned with two sweating glasses of elderflower iced tea, they placed their orders. As she took a sip, Quinn looked around at the deliberately wind-blown customers. Fashionably wrinkled linen, floppy straw hats, nails gleaming with fresh-for-the-weekend mani-pedis.

"So, otherwise, how are you managing?" Leigh asked.

"Mostly, better." She played with the seam of the napkin in her lap and felt her eyes start to tear up. "I still can't believe it sometimes. It's like maybe one day I'll hear his car pull into the garage and he'll be home again. But I know . . . I know." She shook her head. "I finally went through his things."

"That must have been so hard." It was a genuine state-ment of empathy, she could tell from Leigh's face, and it felt nice to be understood. Understood and not rushed.

"It was time—and now maybe you can think more about the future," Leigh added.

So much for empathy. Leigh was who she was and, as her friend, Quinn would have to accept that person.

The waitress returned and set down their plates. She and Leigh had been closer before Harris died and, just as with her other friends, she had kept Leigh at arm's length this past year. It was hard enough without seeing others' sadness and pity, the fear reflected in their eyes at realizing the precariousness of their own sturdily constructed lives.

As they ate and caught up, Leigh shifted the base of her glass of iced tea from one side of her bread plate to the other. "So, since you mentioned being in the city, you know that dinner party I had last week?"

"The one I weaseled out of?"

"That one." Leigh's silver side bangs bounced as she chuckled. "Jonathan was there. He asked me how you were and we chatted for a second about you. Someone said they heard you had been at a . . ."

She cleared her throat. "A . . . club. Olivia's."

Quinn stiffened, her fork halting mid-air, somewhere between her salad and her mouth.

Leigh may have had the wrong name, but she knew. Talk at that dinner—so that's how Jonathan had found her.

"It's not for me to say anything. I just don't want to see you showing up in the gossip columns, that's all."

Quinn couldn't stifle the chortle. "Maybe it will help backlist sales."

"So it's true?"

"Does it matter?"

"No, and yes." Quinn could see in Leigh's eyes it was more yes than no. "I'm concerned. Not only as your agent."

She eyed Quinn's cheek again and arched a suspicious eyebrow.

"I'm fine. But I appreciate you care." Setting her fork and knife down, Quinn continued. "Since we're raising uncomfortable issues, I was hoping we could talk about where we go from here. I've taken time off, and I know the risks if I don't start writing again, which I haven't. I've thought a lot about it since that meeting with Nely."

She adjusted the edge of the napkin, pulling it square across her lap. "I need to cut ties for a while. For an indefinite while."

There.

"Cut ties with *me*?" Leigh asked.

"Not you. With writing. With the career I had. With Devon. I'm working through things, still not very smoothly, and I . . . I don't know what my life is supposed to look like now. I need to figure that out."

She expected she would cry at this point, but she wasn't. In fact, it felt strangely liberating.

"Have you thought about writing about the healing process? I can see your loyal readers—and people who haven't read you yet—being drawn to a candid memoir about what you've faced and how you're working through it. It could be a wonderful way for them to connect with you on a whole other, more personal level."

"You might be right and I'm not ruling out the idea, but this is private. It's too close, and it's too soon. I won't be able to make sense of anything if I write about it in real time—I don't have any perspective yet."

"You used to tell me writing helped you gain perspective, to make sense of things."

"It used to, before. Maybe I will write about it at some point, but for now I need time away. I need to not have an obligation to a publisher. Or to readers. Or to you. Can you talk to Nely, get me released from the contract? Of course, I'll return the advance they've already paid."

"I'm afraid it's not quite that simple. The contract was for three books, and they are going to want all three."

"Well, tell them. Explain the situation again. I can't pull it out of a hat. I'll give back the money—what else can they expect?"

"That you fulfill the three-book contract by delivering the third book."

Their server paused at the table, evidently realizing it wasn't a good time to ask about dessert. Instead, she deftly removed their plates and left.

"Okay, here's the thing. I'm not going to deliver a third book, and I will return whatever money they already paid for it. Since my magic has gone away, I need you to work yours."

With Leigh, sometimes you had to draw a clear line in the sand, and right now Quinn was grateful for the stubbornness—it forced her to clearly state the decision she had danced around in her mind and hesitated to say aloud.

The subtle drop of Leigh's face told Quinn she got it. "So have you thought about what you'll do? I'm asking that as a friend, not your agent."

"To some degree. First, I want to downsize, sell the house. The money will last longer that way and give me time to figure things out."

"I'm shocked to hear you say that—you love that house."

"I do. We did. It felt big before, but now it's a gigantic echo chamber. All that space is full of memories. Happy ones, which just makes me miss him even more."

"Where will you go?"

"Not far. I want to have access to the city, so somewhere else on the island, or maybe the Hudson Valley, not sure yet." She put her hand on Leigh's arm. "I have to meet a good friend for lunch regularly, so it can't be too far."

Now Leigh's eyes looked watery, a rare show of feeling. "I know I've pressured you, but it's only because I know how strong you are. When terrible things happen, we have to keep pressing forward. I hated to see you wallow."

Wallow?

It was hopeless. Leigh would never fully get it, as much as she thought she did. "You've done a lot to try to help, even when I did my best to push you away."

Leigh dabbed her eyes with the corner of her napkin. "Okay, enough. One more thing, though . . ."

The server brought their check, and Leigh put a credit card down without opening the bill folio. "It's on me. You're on a budget now."

As they walked to their cars, Quinn remembered something. "What were you going to tell me right before we got the check?"

Leigh glanced sideways at her with a crafty grin. "The one more thing was . . . You'll say it's too soon, but you know me—I have a thought and I spit it out. Last week at the party, I told you, Jonathan asked how you were. He looked so genuinely concerned, and, I don't know, he seems different.

"More mature. More settled, maybe? Like he's not trying to prove anything anymore. So I thought I would have you two over for dinner one night, at some *future* time when you feel ready. Don't say anything now, just keep the idea in the back of your mind."

A smile crept across Quinn's face as she faced Leigh. "We've been in touch. He's been pretty wonderful, a good friend."

Leigh nodded approvingly at that.

"We have plans for dinner when he's home in a few weeks, actually. Just the *two* of us."

Leigh nudged her with a shoulder as they walked side by side. "Quinn Layborn, sometimes you surprise me. I think that is definitely an avenue worth investigating."

"Oh, really?" A giggle escaped along with the coy question. That last part, she already knew.

12

ENDING A CHAPTER

The breeze off the ocean fluttered his loosely rolled sleeves and shirttails. While his team shot more B roll, he walked along Rio's iconic black and white stone promenade. In a little while, they were all going to meet up for dinner at a palm-fringed restaurant down the beach.

They had wrapped the bulk of the shooting early today. It was hot, everyone was still jetlagged, and he had been distracted.

There were sexy bodies all around him—surfing, playing volleyball, sunbathing, eating, drinking, laughing—but his mind fixated on one body in particular, whose owner was far away.

At a stall with a pyramid of green coconuts piled on the counter, he ordered an *agua de coco* and chatted with the owner while he opened the top with a machete. He removed the small cap, inserted a straw down to the rich, sweet water pooled inside, and handed it to Jonathan.

Coconut in hand, he was about to walk away when, on second thought, he turned back to grab another straw.

Near a stand of palm trees at the edge of the beach, he found an unoccupied bench, balanced the coconut between two slats, and wrestled his phone out of his pocket.

He wished she were here, her hair blowing in the salty breeze, her delicate fingers trying to corral it behind her ears, her lips closing around the straw to taste the nutty sweetness.

Had she ever been to Rio? Where had she traveled? Where did she dream of going? Almost without words, he had gotten to know her so intimately, and yet there still was much more he needed to learn. She had been different with him in the hospital; they had been different with each other. She opened up to him; she slept against him; she smiled. He wanted more of that; he wanted more of her.

———

SHE FELT LIGHTER after her lunch with Leigh last week. Sad, but lighter. She would always feel sad, and that was okay. Grief was, in some upside-down way, a connection to Harris.

But for the first time, she sensed that the sadness might be able to co-exist with other things. It didn't mean she was "moving on," or that she had gained "closure," as people liked to say.

It meant she would find a way forward, her attachment to Harris forever changed but not severed.

This morning she walked along the boardwalk to the beach, found a spot on the sand, and sat to watch a group of surfers. Seeing them had always reminded her how quickly circumstances could change. One minute, they would be standing, riding a wave, balanced, joyful, laughing in the sun. A split-second later, they could be gone from sight—

washed over, thrown under, fighting to find their way to the surface.

Her phone rang from inside her bag. When she pulled it out, Jonathan's face greeted her, his shirt billowing in the wind, his skin tanned.

He held up a green coconut, two straws jutting out the top. "We wrapped for the day about a half-hour ago, so I bought us a drink. Have you tasted it?"

She squinted and shaded her eyes with her hand so she could see him more clearly. "Only from a juice box. I'm guessing it's better fresh."

His laugh was rich, and the skin around his eyes scrunched when he smiled. It was hard to picture him—the man on the phone screen in front of her right now—having an affair, lying to a woman he loved.

We have no reason to lie to each other, he had said to Quinn in the hospital.

She didn't want to be a fool and let herself fall for someone who had cheated, but she also could believe he had changed. The reasons were vastly different, but hadn't she changed too?

Besides, in the trust department, he had proven himself beyond a doubt. She could not have asked silently for those things, could not have done those things with anyone else—that truth she could not ignore.

But moving ahead with Jonathan meant ending a chapter, closing a book.

Harris had given her a sign the other day in the garden, at least that's what she had made of it. He was at peace—she had sensed that so keenly, and he wanted her to be, too. His spirit had given her the gift of a last goodbye, the one they hadn't gotten to say.

Her chest warmed watching Jonathan, a slow radiating warmth from within that mirrored the sun's rays heating her skin. There was no denying the friendship and the caring she felt from him and for him—or their white-hot chemistry.

Even so, she wasn't sure when she would be ready to let someone else fully into her life, into her heart.

"Can I ask you something?" he said between wind gusts.

"Sure."

"Forget it; it's a better topic to talk about in person. By the way, how was that lunch you texted about with Leigh?"

"Lunch was fine. Ask your question." Their relationship, such as it were, had been mostly one-sided. She had given him very little; he deserved more. "Go ahead. Ask."

"Have you been back to Octavia's since, you know, that night?"

Another gust of wind blew between them. She waited for it to subside to speak.

"I guess your silence answers my question."

"Look, Octavia's becoming a friend, a good friend, and I've agreed to help on the club's security committee. There's also a group of members going out to dinner in a few weeks, and I said I would join them. So yes, I'm involved, but not the way you're imagining it."

She could hear the echo of her voice breaking up with those last few words. "Are you there? Can you hear me?"

Silence followed static as their connection dropped.

It was not the best note to end on. She would try to reach him again later; maybe he would be in a better place.

She put the phone back in her bag, gathered her hair behind her head, and laid back, using the purse as a pillow.

The sun warmed her face, her arms, the rest of her body

as she thought about him. His full, rich voice, his teasing smile, his spontaneous laughter, his hands. God, those hands.

Two more weeks before she could have dinner with him suddenly felt like an incredibly long time.

But you're not ready.

A gull squawked and swooped overhead. Down the beach, a little girl ran with a kite. The light shifted. The surfers left the water and loaded their boards into a retro van.

The phone vibrated for a second against the back of her head, and she fished it out of her bag to read the new text.

> Sorry, lost signal. How about we continue the conversation in person? Don't forget—Saturday in two weeks, 7 o'clock. Can't wait to see you. In the meantime, be safe.

> I will, Jonathan, don't worry.
> And yes, to be continued . . .

After "don't worry," she added the flexing bicep emoji and, at the end of the message, the face with the blushing cheeks and unguarded smile, both of which matched her own.

THANK YOU FOR READING! If you enjoyed *Silently*, please consider leaving a review or telling a friend.

You can access the free *Silently Reader & Book Club Guide* on my website, **www.talyablaine.com**.

Want to share more of Quinn and Jonathan's journey?

Their story continues with Book 2 of the Transformation series, *Secretly*.

Turn the page for an Author's Note from me about writing *Silently*—and how to stay in touch.

AUTHOR'S NOTE

Thank you for reading *Silently*. Believe it or not, this story started out as a dream. I woke up and wrote the opening scenes before they faded from memory. It was a short story —Jonathan and Quinn didn't even have names yet.

I set it aside, but my thoughts kept drifting back to it. These two people shared such an incredible intimacy over the course of a single night. How would that night change each of them? Would they see each other again?

I so wanted to know how their story unfolded. Which meant there was only one way to find out.

As you can probably imagine after reading the book, it was not an easy story to bring to the page. Conveying the depth of Quinn's isolation and sorrow, her guilt over desiring another man, Jonathan's challenge to understand how Quinn needed him, why she decided to visit Octavia's —these were among the most difficult threads to write.

But from the start, Quinn and Jonathan's story fought to be told, with their amazing chemistry and potentially deal-breaking issues.

Toward the end, as I wrote the hospital scene—where

he climbs into the bed and brings his forehead to hers, tenderly creating a snug, safe physical and emotional space for them to be totally honest with each other—I realized their story still wasn't finished.

Over the next seven years, I went on to write *Secretly*, and then *Entirely*. If you, too, want to share more of Quinn and Jonathan's journey—including a secret trip to Paris with Octavia and a big wedding to organize on short notice— you'll want to read *Secretly* next. (Whether you buy *Secretly* or request it through your local library, it's best to read the books in order.)

For advance notice of new books, head to my website, **talyablaine.com**, and sign up for my email list. This is the best way to stay in touch.

At my site, you'll also find bonus material, including Reader & Book Club Guides for *Silently* and the other books.

Last but not least, if you enjoyed *Silently*, I'd be thrilled if you'd leave a review or tell a friend about it.

Thank you! Your support means the world.

XO,
Talya

ABOUT THE AUTHOR

A late-blooming romance reader and romance writer, Talya Blaine makes her fiction debut with contemporary erotic romance novel, *Silently*, which *Publisher's Weekly* BookLife Prize Contest reviewers called "a unique work with fascinating characters."

Blaine writes older characters, including strong heroines and sexy, sensitive "beta" heroes, exploring how relationships grow and change with time.

When she's not working at her day job in marketing, she loves to read, write, and blog about steamy romances; hike with her border collie; and spend time with Mr. Blaine, her amazing real-life romance hero.

Learn more at www.talyablaine.com.

ALSO BY TALYA BLAINE

Transformation Series

Silently (Book 1)

"This is a unique work with fascinating characters, drawn together as they individually recover from profound loss." -The BookLife Prize

Secretly **(Book 2)**

"Blaine excels at crafting a plausible plot and ratcheting up the heat and chemistry..."

"Hot and deliciously steamy..." -The BookLife Prize

Entirely **(Book 3)**

"Blaine continues the Transformation series with this third installment, spilling over with steamy bedroom scenes..."

"...the deep interplay between the two main characters adds a special intimacy to the novel." -The BookLife Prize

www.ingramcontent.com/pod-product-compliance
Lightning Source LLC
Chambersburg PA
CBHW021015180626
46814CB00003B/1291